# I Met Murder

# I Met
# Murder

E. X. Ferrars

FELONY & MAYHEM PRESS • NEW YORK

I MET MURDER

A Felony & Mayhem mystery

PRINTING HISTORY
First UK edition (Collins): 1985
First US edition (Doubleday): 1986

Felony & Mayhem edition: 2023

ISBN: 978-1-63194-292-1 (paperback)
978-1-63194-295-2 (ebook)

Manufactured in the United States of America

Cataloging-in-Publication information for this book
is available from the Library of Congress.

The icon above says you're holding a book in the Felony & Mayhem "British" category. These books are set in or around the UK, and feature the highly literate, often witty prose that fans of British mystery demand. If you enjoy this book, you may well like other "British" titles from Felony & Mayhem Press.

———————

For information about British titles or to learn more about Felony & Mayhem Press, please visit us online at:

www.FelonyAndMayhem.com

# Other "British" titles from

## FELONY&MAYHEM

**MICHAEL DAVID ANTHONY**
*The Becket Factor*
*Midnight Come*
*Dark Provenance*

**ROBERT BARNARD**
*Corpse in a Gilded Cage*
*Death and the Chaste Apprentice*
*The Skeleton in the Grass*
*Out of the Blackout*

**SIMON BRETT**
*Blotto, Twinks and the Ex-King's*
  *Daughter*
*Blotto, Twinks and the*
  *Dead Dowager Duchess*
*Blotto, Twinks and the*
  *Rodents of the Riviera*
*Blotto, Twinks and the*
  *Bootlegger's Moll*

**CAROLINE GRAHAM**
*The Killings at Badger's Drift*
*Death of a Hollow Man*
*Death in Disguise*
*Written in Blood*
*Murder at Madingley Grange*

**ELIZABETH IRONSIDE**
*The Accomplice*
*The Art of Deception*
*Death in the Garden*
*A Very Private Enterprise*

**MAGGIE JOEL**
*The Second-Last Woman in*
  *England*
*The Past and Other Lies*

**SHEILA RADLEY**
*Death in the Morning*
*The Chief Inspector's Daughter*
*A Talent for Destruction*
*Fate Worse than Death*

**LESLIE THOMAS**
*Dangerous Davies: The Last*
  *Detective*

**L.C. TYLER**
*The Herring Seller's Apprentice*
*Ten Little Herrings*
*The Herring in the Library*
*Herring on the Nile*
*Crooked Herring*

**E.X. FERRARS**
*Something Wicked*
*Root of All Evil*
*The Crime and the Crystal*
*The Other Devil's Name*
*Last Will and Testament*
*Frog in the Throat*

# I Met Murder

# Chapter One

The obituary in *The Times* on Tuesday morning caught my eye just by chance. I have not yet reached the age when it comes almost automatically to read that column daily to see if any of my friends have dropped by the wayside.

It was the name that caught my attention.

"Sara Noble, peacefully at her home…"

There were some details about the time and place of the funeral and a mention of a loving daughter. Then the next notice went on to give some information about someone else who had died peacefully at her home.

And so, oddly enough, did the one after it. "Peacefully at her home…" "Peacefully at St. Mary's Hospital…" Almost everyone in the column had died peacefully somewhere or other.

But why, I wondered, should the fact need to be mentioned unless it was conceivable that they had died violently? The one statement surely implied the possibility of the other.

I was at breakfast alone in my little house in Allingford when this struck me. I was later than I ought to have been and so was rather in a hurry to get out to my work. Reaching for the coffeepot, I poured out the third cup without which I do not feel really human, and tried to imagine an obituary that began, "Violently at his home, beloved father, etc...."

I had a feeling that this was getting rather close to Hegel. I am very ignorant of philosophy, but I was fairly sure that some good, solid German had stated that anything you say must imply its opposite. However, what I was really thinking about just then was that Sara Noble, famous actress whom I had often admired and who was sure to be widely mourned, was a relation of some friends of mine and that perhaps I ought to telephone and offer sympathy.

If I did it now I was sure to be late at the clinic where I work, part-time, as a physiotherapist, and I was not even sure that it was something that I ought to do at all. Though Sara Noble and my friend, Ann Brightwell, were cousins of some sort, I did not know how distant they were and I had a feeling that there had been some sort of quarrel in the family. So it seemed best to do nothing about the matter. But I had only just stood up and begun to collect my breakfast things to take them out to the kitchen when the telephone rang and it was Ann.

"Virginia, have you seen the notice in *The Times* this morning?" she asked with an excitement in her voice that surprised me.

Ann was fifty, the wife of Hubert Brightwell, a retired Permanent Under Secretary of some ministry or other, and they lived in a big, pleasant Edwardian house on the outskirts of Allingford. By my standards they were very rich people, but I did not actually know in what class of wealth they belonged. In these outspoken days money is still the great conversational taboo. We may tell our friends the most intimate details of our sexual lives, but generally do not think it proper to tell them the size of our incomes. All I knew about the Brightwells was that they were not in the Rolls-Royce and swimming-pool class, but had a Jaguar and a little old Mini in which Ann did her shopping. A Portuguese couple looked after them and they were both always beautifully dressed and were generous donors to local charities. And Hubert of course had a knighthood. At the same time they both seemed to be oddly lonely and unhappy people.

I had become a friend of Ann's when she had been a patient of mine after she had had both hips operated on for arthritis, and it had been after she had made an excellent recovery, yet did not seem to want to part with me, that I had first sensed the loneliness in her that made me sorry for her.

Such a feeling is not really the best basis for a friendship. There is patronage in it and sometimes even some degree of contempt, yet our relationship had survived now for some years, perhaps because I was lonelier myself than I wanted to acknowledge.

"Yes, I saw it," I said. "I was thinking of ringing you up about it, but I didn't know if it would mean much to you."

"*Much!*" she exclaimed. "Of course it does. I'm so excited about it."

That puzzled me. I had never seen any sign of callousness in her and there certainly is some callousness in becoming excited at the death of even a very distant cousin.

"Then it affects you in some way, does it?" I said. I had nearly mentioned the taboo subject of money and asked if she was inheriting something considerable from Sara Noble, because I could not think of any other explanation of Ann's obvious pleasure.

"Well, perhaps not directly," she said. "In fact, at the moment it'll be rather expensive for us, because we shall have to raise the insurance, but there's something so thrilling about it. I'm sure you understand that."

What I was beginning to understand was that we were talking at cross purposes. It seemed probable that the notice in *The Times* about which she was talking was not the obituary of Sara Noble.

"I don't think I do," I said. "I saw the notice of the death of your cousin—"

"Oh, that." She brushed it aside. "D'you know, I never even met her? No, I meant the one about the sale at Christie's."

"Oh," I said. "No, I haven't seen that."

"A Claude Baraud was sold for two hundred and twenty thousand!"

"Oh, I see," I said.

I did begin to see.

She went on swiftly, "He's been nearly forgotten for over a hundred years and now he's being recognized at last. And that means, of course, that the ones we've got are worth ever so much more than we ever dreamt. But it isn't just because of that that I'm so thrilled, as we've no intention of selling them. It's the thought of him being discovered and regarded as he ought to be as one of the great ones. If he hadn't died so young—he was only thirty when he was killed—there'd never have been any question of it. But it's better late than never. After all, he left some wonderful things behind and now justice is being done to him. Not that it doesn't mean some complications for us, as I was saying. The first thing Hubert said when we read about the sale was that we'd have to raise the insurance on our pictures, and then he said that we ought to have special locks put on our doors and windows. I suppose he's right. He knows much more about that sort of thing than I do. The fact is, I can't really take it in yet, but I wanted to talk about it to someone and I knew you'd be interested."

"Well, I do congratulate you," I said. "Baraud was your great-grandfather, wasn't he?"

"My step-great-grandfather actually," Ann answered. "He was my great-grandmother's first husband. She was a Scot, you know, and she went to Paris as a governess and met Claude Baraud there and married him. Then he was killed and she came back to England and married again. But she'd brought most of his pictures with her and that's how it happens that I've got several. Still, that isn't the only thing I wanted to talk to you about, Virginia. I wanted to ask if you would come to lunch with us on Sunday. Hubert's nephew, Tim, and his nice young wife will be there and so will our new neighbour, Clyde Crendon. You haven't met him, have you?"

It should be unnecessary for me to say who Clyde Crendon was. At that time his paperback thrillers decorated every station bookstall. He had recently moved into a small, old, stone-built house near the Brightwells, no one quite knew why, because he could certainly have afforded something far more luxurious.

"No," I said, "I haven't."

"He's such a nice little man," Ann said. "Gentle, unpretentious, rather shy. You'd never dream he's got all that sex and sadism whirling around in his brain. I rather think his publisher may have persuaded him to put it in for the sake of the sales. I'm sure it doesn't come naturally. If you met him without knowing that he was a very successful writer, you'd probably think he was a solicitor, or perhaps a university lecturer, or something like that. I'm sure you'll like him. You'll come, won't you?"

It was worrying me that this conversation already meant that I should be late for my appointment at the clinic, so I said that I should be delighted to accept her invitation and rang off. Ann could go on talking for a long time on the telephone if one did not take a firm line with her.

Going out to my car I wondered if she simply wanted an odd woman at her table to balance the single man, or if she was making another of her rather unfortunate attempts to find me a husband. This is a hazard I have had to face at the hands of other well-meaning friends a number of times since the breakup of my marriage to Felix.

Not that it is quite accurate to call it broken up. He and I have never got around to having a divorce. Three years of marriage had been more than enough for both of us and in the six years that had followed neither of us had reached the point of wanting to repeat the experience. So it had seemed to us both that it would only be a waste of time and money to go to law about it and we still occasionally saw each other, and so long as this did not happen too often I believe we both felt some enjoyment in doing so.

But Ann could not understand this and was sure, however brave a face I put on it, that only a nice husband would cure what must be a deep unhappiness.

I met Clyde Crendon at the Brightwells' house on the Sunday morning and did not think that I would want to marry him. But I liked him and hoped that Ann had not frightened him by telling him too much about my marriage requirements. He was a short man, aged probably about forty, which is slightly younger than I am myself, and though he was not exactly fat, he had a sort of pleasant chubbiness, a round face, smooth pink cheeks, soft, full lips and a high, unlined forehead. His rather sparse hair was straw-coloured and his eyes were grey. Not a man you would notice if you passed him in the street. Yet there was something about his eyes which gradually made an impression on me. They were more watchful, more thoughtful than altogether fitted his kind of face. But that did not dawn on me immediately, partly because, when we first met, which was in the Brightwells' hall, his attention was focused entirely on the Claude Baraud painting that hung on the wall opposite the front door.

Ann had hurried out to greet me when Santos, the Portuguese manservant, had let me in. She introduced me to Clyde Crendon, then wanted to sweep us both into her drawing room, but he lingered, turning back to gaze at the picture and to say with a sigh, "It really is a lovely thing, isn't it?"

I had always thought so myself, without knowing anything about its value. There was an extraordinary sense of quiet about it, of remote distances and yet of friendly intimacy. I knew that it was called *Le Repas en plein air*. It was a picture of a group of Victorian ladies and gentlemen having a picnic. The men wore straw boaters, the women pretty bonnets. In the distance were far-off mountains, to be seen beyond a group of tall trees, and in the foreground there was a luxurious tangle of wild flowers.

The figures looked relaxed and contentedly at ease. They were seated on benches at a rough wooden table, with bottles of wine and glasses before them. You could almost feel the warmth of the sunshine in the air. It was a big picture in a heavy frame and, except for a pretty little Sheraton side table with a bowl of daffodils on it, was the only object in the square, lofty hall.

Gazing at the picture as if he could not tear himself away from it, Clyde Crendon said, "Do you know Degas once said that a painting requires as much cunning as the perpetration of a crime?"

Then reluctantly he let himself be drawn after me into the drawing room.

Like the hall, it had a high ceiling which had some mock-Tudor beams in it, and an imitation Adam fireplace which did not really agree too well with the beams. There were plentiful cretonne-covered sofas and chairs and two more Claude Baraud paintings, one on each side of the fireplace. One was of a vase of dahlias and the other of a woman with her head bent over some embroidery. I am too ignorant to be able to describe them adequately, but it had always seemed to me that they had the same sense of peace and brightness that there was in the greater painting in the hall.

"You've met Tim and Barbie, haven't you, Virginia?" Ann said to me. "But I don't think you have, Mr. Crendon. My husband's nephew and his wife, Mr. and Mrs. Halliday."

Ann was a tall woman, slender and narrow-shouldered, with a slight stoop which in some way exaggerated an air of diffidence she had, as if she hoped that it would help her to crouch unobserved in whatever company she found herself. Yet she was a social woman, fond of going to parties and even more of giving them, and taking a responsible part in good works in the town. But it had always seemed to me that she did this not because the causes interested her, but because it kept her in contact with other people, saving her from having to be alone with herself.

She had a pointed face and fine, delicate features, more wrinkled than they ought to have been at fifty, as if by some inner tension. She had short, straight grey hair, docked in a fringe across her forehead, and hazel eyes, full of an anxious eagerness that she should be liked. She was wearing one of her very simple, distinguished-looking dresses in a soft shade of grey.

Tim and Barbie Halliday both kissed me, then shook hands with Clyde Crendon. Tim was a tall, dark young man of about thirty, with a long, thin face, a chronic frown and an odd, crooked smile. If you like them dark and sardonic, you would have thought him very good-looking. He was a journalist, the assistant editor of a monthly magazine called *The Platform*, and lived in London, though he and Barbie had a small cottage a few miles out of Allingford. She was two or three years younger than he was and was small, slim, and lively, with a mop of blond curls, a small, rosy face and sparkling blue eyes which could change in a moment from a look of gay innocence to one of disconcerting shrewdness. She also worked on *The Platform*, editing their women's page, which was a very superior sort of women's page that had no truck with fashions or cookery and never gave advice on how to keep your boyfriend, but was mostly devoted to women's rights and questions concerning contraception, abortion, divorce, and progressive forms of education for the young. I thought she probably dominated Tim, though she was clever enough not to show it. She was in a dark red tweed suit, wore long, dangling earrings and shoes with very high heels.

"My husband's in the garden," Ann said. "I'll call him."

Going to the French window at one end of the room, she opened it and called out, "Hubert!"

A distant cry answered her.

Turning back into the room, she went on, "He'll be in in a moment. Are you a keen gardener too, Mr. Crendon? Hubert couldn't bear to spend such a lovely morning indoors."

It was a very lovely morning. The sky was a cloudless blue and sunshine lay brilliantly across the wide lawn at the back of the house and made the golden forsythia at the bottom of the garden glitter. There was a slight breeze that stirred the daffodils along the edges of the lawn. Buds were swelling on the flowering cherries. The garden was a conventionally suburban one, but at that time of the year and on such a morning could hardly have been anything but beautiful.

"I shall try my hand at it, now that I've got a garden of my own," Clyde Crendon said. "I've always lived in flats ever since I grew up. But at the moment I can't think of anything but your wonderful pictures, Lady Brightwell. Would it be impertinent to ask how they came into your possession?"

"I inherited them," Ann said. "Claude Baraud was my great-grandmother's first husband."

We had all sat down and Tim was pouring out drinks.

"Then you aren't actually descended from him yourself," Clyde Crendon said. "Did he have no children?"

"No, he died only a few months after he married my great-grandmother," Ann answered. "He was called up when the Franco-Prussian war broke out and he was killed at the battle of Beaune-la-Rolande. Before that he'd been working in the Atelier Gleyre where he met Monet and Renoir and Bazille and Sisley. They all used to go painting together in the forest at Fontainebleau. He came of good Protestant bourgeois stock in Lyon and went to Paris to study law, but that didn't last long. After his death my great-grandmother came home and two or three years later married my great-grandfather and they had two daughters, one of whom was my grandmother. And some of Claude Baraud's paintings, which my great-grandmother had brought home with her, came down to my grandmother, and so to my mother, and in the end to me. Not that I think they were ever appreciated as they ought to have been until they got into my hands, and I have to confess that I'd no conception of their value till I read about the sale at Christie's. I always loved them, but mainly I treasured them because they were a sort of family thing."

"What happened to the other daughter?" Clyde Crendon asked. "Your grandaunt, that would have been."

"Oh, she married and had a daughter," Ann said. "I don't actually know much about that side of the family, because there was a bitter quarrel between my mother and her cousin. They'd been brought up together, almost like sisters, but there was some trouble about a man. I believe he was engaged to my mother, or she thought he was, then he suddenly went off and married her cousin. My mother, of course, married someone else, my father, but she never forgave her cousin. She had a daughter. You'll know her name. She was Sara Noble, the actress who died the other day, but I never met her."

"Did you never try to?" Clyde Crendon asked.

"As a matter of fact, I did," Ann said. "When I grew up I thought it was a pity to let a quarrel of that sort linger on and I wrote to her, suggesting we might meet, but I never had an answer. I don't know if it was still because of the quarrel, or if it was because she thought I only wanted to patch it up because she'd become famous. In fact, that had made me hesitant about writing, because I didn't want her to think anything of that sort. In any case, nothing came of it."

"She'd a daughter, hadn't she?" I said. "There was something about a loving daughter in that notice in *The Times*."

"Yes, but there was no sign of her in the television pictures of the funeral yesterday," Barbie said. "But of course there were a lot of celebrities there, so she may have got obscured."

"There was no mention of a husband either," Tim said. "What happened to him, d'you know?"

"I don't think there ever was a husband," Ann answered. "Holly—that's the girl's name—is illegitimate, or so I believe from something I read about Sara Noble somewhere or other."

"And the girl's been in trouble already," Tim said, "and I believe she's only sixteen or thereabouts. Don't you remember a year or so ago she was arrested at a party with some other kids for being in possession of cannabis? Of course it wouldn't have got into the papers if she hadn't been Sara Noble's daughter, but it was given a good deal of publicity. I wonder what's going to happen to her now."

"I don't know…" Ann began, but was interrupted by the appearance of Hubert at the French window.

❋ ❋ ❋

He came in and gave me the normal kiss of greeting, then shook hands with Clyde Crendon.

Hubert was a not very well-preserved sixty, tall, wide-shouldered, heavily built, with a considerable paunch which he seemed to feel an effort to thrust around before him, for he often had attacks of breathlessness, as if the weight of it were a little too much for him. He had short, upstanding grey hair, a large face with several chins and small, red-veined eyes with pouches under them that gave him the melancholy look of some kind of hound. He had a firm, tight-lipped mouth. His manner was ponderous, generally amiable but could easily become petulant if his self-importance was challenged. He had decided opinions about most things, but was a kind man, generous and affectionate. Although he often seemed to bully Ann, I was inclined to think that he loved her more than she did him.

After helping himself to a drink, he sat down with his thick legs sprawling in one of the cretonne-covered chairs. He was wearing a heavy pullover and aged trousers, frayed at the turn-ups and dotted here and there with the burrs of sticky willie, which I supposed he had been rooting up.

"I heard you talking about that child, Holly," he said. "Sara's kid. No good, we know that much about her. But Ann's got it into her head—"

"Please!" Ann interrupted. "Let's not talk about it now."

"Why not?" he asked. "See what these people think about your idea. As I was saying—"

"Please, Hubert—we don't want an argument now, do we?" she said swiftly.

"Who's said anything about an argument?" He sipped his whiskey. "No need for one, is there? I'd just like to know how your idea strikes other people. It may not seem as crazy to them as it does to me. If it doesn't, I'll admit I may have been mistaken. What's wrong with that? I hope I'm always ready to listen to other people."

"Darling Uncle Hubert, of course you listen to them except when you feel like talking them down," Barbie said. "And even when you don't, it doesn't mean you're going to take much notice of what they say."

He guffawed. She was a great favourite with him.

"That's unkind, Barbie dear," he said. "I'm the most tolerant of men. I never shrink from criticism. And if in the present instance I'm wrong and the matter is one which will seriously affect Ann's happiness, of course she shall have her way."

Ann gave a sigh. "I still think it's a private matter which I'd much prefer to think over by myself before doing any talking about it. But if you insist, go ahead."

Clyde Crendon gave a little cough, drawing attention to himself.

"If we might return to Claude Baraud for a moment…"

His round, pink face was bland, but he had done it, I was sure, to extricate Ann from a position which for some reason she found embarrassing. I decided that I must buy one of his books and find out if they were really as brutally sadistic as I had been told.

"Ah!" Hubert said, his attention easily deflected. "That's another matter on which Ann and I don't see eye to eye. Now that we know how valuable the pictures are, I think we ought to sell them. Not just for the cash, though I don't despise that, but to be free of the worry of having them in the house. But Ann won't hear of it and I must say I understand her point of view. They're family heirlooms and all that, so of course she's got feelings about them. And I dare say if we keep them they'll turn out a good investment. In another couple of years they may be selling for half a million. But it's a worry at the moment that of course we've got to have new locks on the doors and windows. I don't know much about such things, but I believe one can get advice from the police about it, and in any case I'm going up to London next week to talk to a friend who's got a valuable collection of jade in his house and who's gone into the question of security very thoroughly. He'll tell me what I should do and whom I should go to to get the job done. But then, of course, there's the insurance, too. God knows what that'll come to. They tell me that in art galleries they don't insure the pictures at all because they can't afford the premiums, so that people who steal the pictures and expect to get a ransom for them are disappointed."

The door opened and Santos came in to tell us that luncheon was served.

We had salmon and new potatoes, an apple pie and cream, and a pleasant white wine.

I was on Hubert's right, with Tim on the other side of me and as he and I began to chat I had a feeling that something was amusing him. This did not dispel his heavy frown, in fact, if anything, it seemed to make him twitch his eyebrows more formidably together than usual, as if he were trying to control something that made him want to laugh outright.

I began to have an uncomfortable feeling that it was something about me and after a little while I asked him, "What's the joke, Tim?"

"Joke?" he said. "Is there one?"

"You look as if there were."

He shook his head. "I'm sorry. Of course there's my uncle's bright idea, which I admit amuses me, but I didn't think it showed. Tell me, have you seen Felix lately?"

I knew that Tim and my husband were acquainted, though not very intimately. But I did not want to talk about Felix. I very seldom do.

"Not for quite a while," I said.

"And you haven't heard from him, either?"

"No."

"You don't know what he's doing?"

"When I last saw him he was running a marriage bureau called Sunset Love. I believe it was quite successful. But it wouldn't surprise me if he's given it up. He never sticks to anything. What's this bright idea of Hubert's you mentioned, or is it something it's best not to talk about, like Ann's?"

I did not intend Hubert to hear me, but unfortunately he did.

"Ah yes, Ann's idea, let's go back to that," he said. "I don't see why she should make such a fuss about talking it over among a few friends. It's simply that we should offer that child Holly a home. I think it's ridiculous myself. The idea that a girl who's grown up in the theatrical world, at the top of it, too, and who's already been in trouble for smoking pot and heaven knows what else, would think of coming to live in a place like Allingford with two old fogies like us—can you imagine it?"

I had never thought of Ann as an old fogy, though perhaps the description applied fairly aptly to Hubert. All the same, I was inclined to agree with him that the daughter of Sara Noble would not even consider making her home with the Brightwells.

But there were almost tears in Ann's voice as she said, "You've put it all wrong. I've never said anything about asking her to come to live with us. I only said that as she's so young and hasn't got a father, we ought to try to find out what her situation is—there must be a family lawyer who can tell us that—and if she's really alone in the world, we might suggest to her that she should stay with us for a while, till she's made up her mind about what she wants to make of her life. And I quite realize the suggestion may not appeal to her in the least. She may have friends who are looking after her, or for all we know she may have gone on the stage already herself. But I can't see what harm there would be in inviting her to come to us for a time. She can easily refuse."

"Except that you'll be brokenhearted if she does," Hubert said, and I thought he was genuinely concerned that Ann might be badly hurt. "Don't try to deceive yourself, what you want is to adopt her. Haven't we gone over that sort of thing again and again? And haven't you agreed with me that the risks of adoption are very great? You can't know anything to speak of about the heredity of the child. The parents may be idiots or criminals. Chances are they're one or the other, or why aren't they taking responsibility for the child themselves?"

"Sara Noble wasn't an idiot or a criminal," Ann said. "She was an immensely gifted woman."

"But she had an illegitimate child, and what do we know about the father?" Hubert asked.

The atmosphere was becoming distinctly uncomfortable. Ann had flushed and there was a suspicious brightness in her eyes. Hubert was looking complacent and determined. But again Clyde Crendon intervened.

"I do agree with you, Lady Brightwell, that Sara Noble was something outstanding," he said. "I never missed a film of hers if I could help it, and I went to see her Lady Macbeth three times in a month when she and Roger Cairns were in it together. I don't know how many times I've seen that play, but that's the best performance of it I can remember. Of course, she outshone him. I believe if I were in Lady Brightwell's place I'd feel very inclined to see if I could make friends with her daughter. If she has any of her mother's qualities it should be a very exciting experience."

Hubert looked as if he would have liked to tell the little man that he did not see what business of his it was to offer advice on the matter, but he was too courteous to say so.

Ann's face lit up with a sweet smile. I felt very sorry for her. I had found out long ago how desperately she wanted a child and I knew that she and Hubert had argued on and on through the years about the question of adoption. My sympathies had always been with her, but I thought that in this case Hubert was almost certainly right that for her to set her heart on making a home for a girl with Holly Noble's background would be hopeless folly.

I turned back to Tim.

"You still haven't told me what Hubert's bright idea is," I said.

"Only that he's decided to write his autobiography," Tim answered. "A very suitable occupation for elderly gentlemen, of course, but I can't help finding it comic. I've promised Barbie that if I survive to the age when the urge seems to hit people, I'll never write mine."

Hubert had again overheard what had not been meant for his ears.

"Comic? What's comic about it?" he demanded. "I've led a very interesting life. My childhood in India—people are getting interested in those days again—then the war years, my experiences as a commando, and then my struggle to establish myself in the jungle of the Civil Service. I don't see how it can fail. And

I've got hold of a very good secretary, at least, I suppose he's good, since you got him for me yourself, Tim. And as you know, I'm not afraid of hard work. It will be hard work, of course. I know that. But I've made up my mind to begin tomorrow.

"Well, good luck to you, uncle," Tim said, "but I'm afraid you may find it more difficult than you expect to get words down on paper."

"I've never been afraid of facing difficulties," Hubert replied rather pompously. "You mean, of course, that I've never tried my hand at writing before. But I don't see why I shouldn't be able to do it if other people can. Don't you agree, Crendon? You should know."

I was sure that Clyde Crendon did not agree in the least, but he gave his amiable smile and said, "Why not?" He turned to Ann again. "If that child Holly does come here, I'd so much like to meet her. You say you never have."

"No, and I don't even know where she's living at the moment," Ann said, "but we can find that out. I'm so glad you agree with me about her, Mr. Crendon." She gave a glance of triumph at Hubert, as if the fact that her well-known neighbour was on her side naturally won the battle for her.

Presently we returned to the drawing room for coffee. I sat down on a sofa and Clyde Crendon came to sit beside me. Though his attention was obviously on the Baraud painting of the woman bending over her embroidery, he worked at making conversation with me.

"Have you lived in Allingford for a long time, Mrs. Freer?" he asked.

"I grew up here," I answered.

"And you've always lived here?"

"Well, I went away for a time, but it wasn't for long," I said. "Fortunately when I came back they gave me my old job again and I lived with my mother. Then when she died she left me her house and I still live in it."

"You must like it very much."

"I do."

I did not see any need to explain to him that the time that I had spent away from Allingford was the three years which I had spent trying to keep my marriage to Felix from falling apart, though that had been something that I ought to have seen, after six months, would be impossible.

"What brought you here?" I asked.

"Love," he answered. "Love at first sight. I fell head over heels in love with a house. I was with some friends who drove me past it and I saw the 'For Sale' sign at the gate and something went click in my brain and I insisted on stopping and seeing over it, and I made an offer for it next day."

"And you haven't regretted it?"

"Not for a moment. I find it much easier to work here than I do in London. I've kept my flat there, but I find myself spending more and more time down here. The quiet suits me. I hadn't realized before how much I needed it. And my neighbours are very nice people. Lady Brightwell particularly has been very kind. She found me a splendid housekeeper who looks after me to perfection."

"Do you often do that sort of thing?" I asked. "I mean, see a 'For Sale' sign and make an immediate offer."

"I believe I do," he said. "Yes, since you ask me, I believe I do. For instance, if there were a 'For Sale' sign on any of these Baraud paintings, I'd offer Lady Brightwell here and now whatever she liked to ask for them. But I understand it wouldn't be much use, so I shan't trouble her about it. And of course, she's right to keep them."

"As an investment?"

"No, no, no, because of their beauty. You know, there aren't very many people who have the privilege of owning really beautiful things. Nice things, pretty things, odds and ends that have caught our fancy, we all have those, but truly beautiful things belong to so very few." He gave a sigh and passed a hand over his high, unlined forehead as if to brush away a disturbing thought, then turned to chat to Tim, who had sat down near him.

As if he felt sure that the author would expect it, Tim started to question him about his work, asking him how long it took him to write a book, how many he had written, where his ideas came from, whether he worked regular hours or only when he felt like it, and all the other questions that a writer friend of mine tells me that writers are invariably asked.

Clyde Crendon answered him patiently and courteously, but was obviously glad when Ann suggested that she should show him round the garden.

Tim and Barbie drove me home. The spring morning had been so fine that I had walked to the Brightwells' house instead of driving, but I was glad enough of the lift home. By car it took only a few minutes.

Tim asked me what I thought of Clyde Crendon and I replied that I had liked him.

When Tim said nothing to this, I said, "Don't you?"

"Do I like him? Yes, oh yes, of course," Tim answered a little too hurriedly. "Nothing to dislike, is there?"

"I wouldn't be too sure of that," Barbie said. "Those books of his…" She gave a sharp little shudder.

I wondered if the trouble might be that Tim and Barbie, both journalists and far from prosperous, were jealous of a man who was as successful as Clyde Crendon.

"I'll try reading one of them sometime soon," I said. "But tell me, will that autobiography of Hubert's ever get written?"

For some reason this sent both of them into fits of laughter. "I think that depends on the secretary we got for him," Tim replied.

"Tell her," Barbie said. "Go on and tell her."

"No, let her find it out for herself," Tim said.

I found it very puzzling. I only discovered what they meant after they had put me down at my gate and I had let myself in at my front door. Even then I did not discover it immediately, but what I noticed at once as I went towards the sitting room was that there was a strong smell of tobacco smoke in the air, and as I have not smoked for ten years it meant that I had a visitor.

And there was only one person who could let himself into the house in my absence. Felix was there.

I found him lying on the sofa with a cigarette in one hand and a heap of ash and cigarette ends in a saucer on the floor beside him. He did not get to his feet when I entered, which was unlike him, because he has very good manners, and it took me a moment to understand the reason. It was simply that all that I could see of his right leg was encased in plaster.

# Chapter Two

He said, "I could get up but it would take me a long time."

Twitching up his trouser leg, he showed me that the plaster went up to his knee.

"What's the trouble?" I asked.

"Broken," he answered. "My tibula."

"There's no such bone in the human body," I said. "It's either your tibia or your fibula."

"It feels like both," he said. "In any case, it's my bloody shinbone."

"How did it happen?"

"You might at least say you're sorry for me."

"I'm very sorry, but I'm curious too. And I'm curious about what you're doing here and how you got here in the state you're in."

He lit another cigarette from the stub of the last one and puffed smoke at me, as if he felt the need of some screen between us.

He looked more haggard than usual, I supposed because of his injury. All the same, he was wearing very well. At forty-two he was as good-looking as he had been when we married, perhaps even more so. Boyish charm, which had lasted well into his thirties, had yielded to an air of distinction, assisted by the threads of grey in his fair hair. He would soon be able to call himself perhaps Professor Freer, or tell people that he held an important post in the Ministry of Defence where he worked on matters so secret that they could not fail to be impressed, or that he was a merchant banker who just happened, most unfortunately, to have left his wallet at home and so would be very grateful for a small loan from them. I wondered what role he was playing now, or if the truth was that he was simply unemployed and had descended on me for assistance.

He was of medium height and slender, with an almost triangular face, wide at the temples, pointed at the chin, with curiously drooping eyelids that made his vivid blue eyes look almost triangular too.

"To take one thing at a time," he said, "it was some unspeakable kid on a bicycle. I'm old-fashioned enough to believe that pavements are meant for pedestrians and I haven't got used to the fact that the young treat them as cycle tracks. I've trained myself to look out for perambulators and people with shopping trolleys trailing behind them and I've never yet fallen over one of them, but I can't get used to the fact that kids come belting along on pavements on bicycles without even tinkling a bell when they see a pedestrian in danger. Anyway, do bicycles have bells at all nowadays? I can't think how many years it is since I last heard one."

"So one of these children ran into you," I said.

I stooped to add some coal to the fire. I had banked it up well before I left but it was nearly out now. However, the sunshine had been pouring in at the window since early in the morning and the room was comfortably warm.

It was a room I liked, though there was nothing special about it. It had furniture of several periods in it that my mother had assembled little by little during the time that she had lived there and which I had left as she had arranged it. There were several comfortable chairs, some unremarkable pictures, and a bay window at one end that overlooked my small garden in which at the moment an almond tree was in blossom.

"I wonder if you have to work hard at sounding so unsympathetic whenever you talk to me," Felix said, "or if it just comes naturally when you're talking to other people too."

"I said I was sorry, didn't I?" I said. I sat down in a chair facing him across the hearth. "Was the child hurt too?"

"I hope so. I was walking calmly along when something in a shopwindow caught my eye and I stepped sideways to look at it without remembering that I ought to look behind me before doing something so reckless, and so I walked smack into this subhuman fiend on a bicycle. And the next thing was that someone with some sense called an ambulance and I was stuck in hospital for the rest of the day."

"And I suppose it's been pretty difficult for you to look after yourself in the flat," I said, "and that's why you're here."

"Well, no, it isn't."

Since I had left him, Felix had continued to live in the flat in Little Carberry Street which we had occupied for the three years that we had stayed together, and normally he was capable of looking after himself very well. He was an admirably domesticated man, very tidy and an excellent cook. But with a broken leg it would be another matter. The flat was on the first floor of the house and merely to go shopping for food would mean negotiating a long flight of stairs down to the street and later climbing them again, which would be difficult and painful.

It was not unlikely, of course, that his neighbours had been helping him. Felix was a very friendly man and normally was on good terms with the people who occupied the other flats in the shabby old Georgian house where he lived. All the same, trying to manage by himself would have been pretty wretched.

"It isn't why you're here?" I said.

"Well, only partly. I admit I thought you might take me in for a time, but my real reason for coming to Allingford is that I've got a job here."

"A new job?"

"Yes."

"But I thought you were doing so well with that marriage bureau of yours."

"I was, and that's why I got a splendid offer for it from a man I know and decided to take it. Actually, I was getting rather bored with it. And disillusioned, too. Sometimes I felt it was little short of pimping. And I thought it would be rather nice to have a lump sum of money for once and perhaps use it to see a little of the world before I got too old to enjoy it."

"You've plenty of time. There are people who still enjoy travelling when they're in their eighties."

"Oh, I know, but I was thinking of looking for jobs here and there and really getting to know the places and the people, not just tourism."

"And you only got as far as Allingford. Poor Felix."

He gave me his three-cornered smile. "It's not much use trying to work one's way round the world with a broken leg. And then I was offered this job here and I admit it was in its favour that I thought you might be ready to put me up, at least till I find some other lodging. After all, we never actually quarrelled, did we?"

My memory of our marriage was that we had hardly ever done anything else, but I knew that Felix was capable of having genuinely blotted this from his mind. For one thing, he had never been able to understand why I had left him. It had been simply because I had not been able to endure living in his strange world of fantasy. He did not understand how much it had hurt me to discover what lies he told about himself. He thought it was very unreasonable of me. To lie, normally making himself out to be far more important than he was and giving himself a far more colourful past than he had had, came to him so naturally that I am inclined to believe he thought it was normal behaviour in everyone.

For instance, when we got married he had told me that he was a civil engineer, working for a big construction firm, when the truth was, as I discovered later by chance, that they had never heard of him and that he was actually working for a very shady firm of secondhand car dealers.

"All right, you can stay here as long as you need to," I said. "Would you like some tea?"

"That's the nicest thing you've said to me since you came in," he said. "I should like some very much."

"But what's this job?" I asked. "Since you can't walk much, I suppose it's something sedentary."

"Yes, though I can get around fairly well on the level," he answered. He pointed to a pair of aluminium crutches that I had already noticed on the floor beside the sofa. "I'm getting quite skilled with those. As a matter of fact, I've been in your kitchen to get myself some lunch. Only some bread and cheese and coffee. I didn't think you'd mind. And I found your whiskey. I don't often drink at midday, as you know, but the journey had rather shaken me up and I needed something for once."

Felix, as a matter of fact, had always drunk very moderately and thought that I drank too much. He was afraid, I used to think, that if he had a drink too many he might become confused in the fictions with which he was living at the time. It must have taken quite an effort of concentration to keep them tidily sorted out.

"About that job," I said, "what is it?"

"Well, I'm going to be a sort of secretary to an old chap who's going to write his autobiography. He's an uncle of Tim Halliday's whom I think you know, and Tim got me the job. He knew I was looking for something to fill in the time while this leg mended. Nice of him, wasn't it? And he and Barbie drove me down here today. The man's name's Brightwell. You do know him, don't you?"

I began to laugh. "Now I know what was amusing Tim and Barbie so much when they drove me home. They knew I was going to find you here and they knew what I was going to think about your taking on a job with poor old Hubert. Honestly, Felix, whatever made you take it? You don't know the first thing about a secretary's work."

"I can type very well," he answered stiffly.

"There's a good deal more to it than that."

"Well, I understand he'll be recording most of his stuff on tape and I'll just have to work it up from that. I shan't need shorthand. To be precise, though I don't think he'd like my saying it, I think I'll be more of a ghost than a secretary."

"But that's even worse. It must take quite a lot of skill to be a successful ghost."

"I don't see why it should need more than normal intelligence."

"It must need at least some talent for writing."

"And how do you know I haven't got it? I've never tried my hand at it before."

This was true. Perhaps it would turn out that he had found a vocation. That would be funny, but who could tell with Felix?

"I don't want to discourage you," I said, "and your employer, with whom I happen to have been having lunch today, probably knows as little about writing as you do, so he may not catch you out for some time."

"You do know him then."

"Oh yes, quite well. His wife and I are close friends."

"Then you can tell me if there's anything special about him it might help me to know."

"I'll do my best. But I'll get the tea first."

I left him to go out to the kitchen, made the tea, put some biscuits on a plate, and carried the tray back to the sitting room. I found that he had sat up, though he had kept his damaged leg stretched out along the sofa. Pulling a coffee table close to him, I put the tray down on it and poured out tea for us both. He was watching me thoughtfully.

"You can be honest with me, you know," he said. "Do you mind the way I've descended on you? If you do, I can go to a hotel till I've found lodgings of some sort."

"It's all right, you can stay," I said, "at least for the present." I knew that he had known that I would say that and that there was no risk that I would turn him out. "But what are you going to do about getting to the Brightwells and back, because I suppose you'll be working at their house and it's much too far for you to walk."

"I rather thought you mightn't mind driving me there in the morning and perhaps picking me up in the evening and bringing me back here, anyway for the first few days till perhaps I can fix up something with some hired-car people. But I don't want to impose on you."

He had had it all mapped out, of course, probably from the time that Tim had first suggested to him that he might take on the job of work for Hubert. Felix had realized at once how convenient it would be to have an ex-wife living in the neighbourhood, a wife with whom he might not be on the best of terms but who was hardly likely to cast him out in his crippled state.

"I see," I said. "All right. After all, the job may not last very long. Hubert may find you out, or he may find himself out. I mean, he may discover the job needs more talent than he expects. Whatever happens, it's going to be a case of the blind leading the blind."

"So that's settled. Thank you. You're being very nice about it all, Virginia. I'm very grateful. And I brought you a small present." He was fumbling in a pocket. "I didn't think I'd give it you till I knew if you were going to be furious with me or not. I mean, I didn't want it to look as if I was trying to bribe you. But here it is and I hope you like it."

He brought a small package wrapped in tissue paper out of his pocket and handed it to me.

I am deadly scared of presents from Felix. I really do not like the feeling of being a receiver of stolen property, even though I believe this is not an offence unless one is aware that the goods in question have been stolen. But the chances were, as I had discovered early in our marriage, that any present given to me by Felix had been annexed by him quietly in some shop when no one was looking and certainly not paid for.

He was an incurable kleptomaniac, if that is the right description of someone who seems to find it a kind of sport to steal little articles that have caught his fancy and for which he could easily afford to pay. He hardly ever kept the things he stole for himself, because he loved giving presents and was thought of by most of his friends as a touchingly generous man.

I unwrapped the package and found a chain of many-coloured agate beads, a very pretty thing.

He was watching me anxiously.

"Go on," he said. "Put it on. It'll go nicely with that blouse you're wearing."

It did and I hesitated only a moment before I fastened it round my neck. It would be useless to try to find out if he had paid for it or not, because he would swear that he had and this might even be true. Occasionally he did pay for what he wanted, so you could never be quite sure where you were with him.

"Thank you," I said.

"You like it?"

"Very much."

"Good, I'm glad you do. Now go on and tell me about these friends of yours. They're nice, are they?"

"I like them. But I think you're going to find them in rather a state of turmoil at present. Hubert may not be able to keep his mind on his work at first. For one thing, they've just discovered that some pictures of theirs which have come down Ann's family to her, and which they've always taken for granted, are very valuable, so they've got to have special locks put on the doors and windows to keep out thieves. And they're going to have to spend some fabulous sum on insurance. So Hubert would like to sell the pictures, but Ann won't hear of it. And for another thing, they're quarrelling about whether or not to invite a girl to stay with them who's some sort of distant cousin of Ann's and who happens to be the daughter of Sara Noble, who died the other day. Ann wants it very badly and obviously hopes it'll lead to their more or less adopting the girl, and Hubert's dead against it."

"You don't make it sound exactly like an ideal marriage."

"Oh, I think it's a fairly good one in its way."

"This Noble girl, do they know her well?"

"I gather they've never met her and they aren't even sure where she is at present. Did you ever see her mother act, Felix?"

"Lord, yes. She was wonderful. Not so good in films, because she seldom had material that was worthy of her and she used to walk through them as if she was too bored for words. But in the theatre she was splendid. I saw her as a really spine-chilling Lady Macbeth. James Calvin was Macbeth, but she overshadowed him completely."

"I thought Roger Cairns was Macbeth. That's what Clyde Crendon said. He was at lunch with the Brightwells today."

Felix shook his head. "I don't think so. I believe Cairns was supposed to be a lover of hers at one time. That's probably how Crendon got it mixed up. Has it ever struck you, by the way, that the Macbeths were the only happy marriage Shakespeare ever wrote about? It's a great thing in marriage to have a common interest. About those pictures, who's the artist?"

"Claude Baraud."

"Never heard of him."

"You will. He's coming into fashion. A picture of his sold at Christie's the other day for a huge sum. He was a friend of Monet and that lot, but he was killed in battle when he was only thirty and got forgotten till recently."

"And will that make a lot of difference to the Brightwells? I mean, are they short of cash? Sir Hubert isn't writing that autobiography because he needs the money, is he? I rather gathered from Tim that they are fairly wealthy."

"I think they are."

"I needn't be afraid I won't get my fee?"

I laughed at the idea of my worthy friends failing to pay Felix anything that they owed him.

"I'm quite sure you needn't."

"Good," he said. "Good. It's nice to know one can rely on people."

I drove him to the Brightwells' house next morning. Using his crutches, he was fairly mobile, but I had made up a bed for him on the divan in my sitting room, and there was a small shower room on the ground floor, so that he did not have to climb the stairs. It gave me a strange feeling to have him staying with me. I no longer felt that he had ever been my husband. It was more as if a friend who had been abroad for some years and of whom I was really quite fond had come to visit me.

But I was not sure how much of this I ought to try to explain to the Brightwells. I had said very little, even to Ann, about my marriage, but I knew that she had made up her mind that Felix was a brutal, faithless man whom it had been angelic of me to attempt to save from his evil ways, while Hubert, with some embarrassment, had always done his best to avoid the subject entirely. So it was no little problem how I ought to introduce Felix to them.

Arriving at the house and being admitted by Santos, I decided to say as little about the situation as possible. So when Ann came hurrying down the stairs to meet me and saw Felix limping behind me, I simply said, "Hallo, Ann, I'm just delivering Hubert's new secretary to him. He happens to be my husband, Felix, who's staying with me for the present. I'll pick him up in the evening. I do hope he'll satisfy Hubert. Now I must rush. I'm late for an appointment already."

Before Ann could say anything, I escaped, leaving her and Felix to cope with one another.

As they were both courteous people, I thought the chances were that nothing too unfortunate would happen. For some reason, once I was in my car and driving to the clinic, I started to laugh and could not stop.

Actually it was an effect that Felix had often had upon me.

❀ ❀ ❀

I picked him up in the evening about half past five. Ann had obviously been waiting for me and insisted on my coming in for a drink. As neither Hubert nor Felix was in the drawing room I assumed that they must still be at work. There was a flush on

Ann's rather lined face and her eyes, which often looked anxious and evasive, were sparkling.

"Virginia, I've just been talking to Holly—isn't it exciting?" she exclaimed as she poured out whiskey for me. "Hubert found out from a friend in the theatre who the Noble family's lawyers were, and we got Holly's telephone number from them, and she wants to come and visit us and she sounds so nice."

"Where is she?" I asked. "In London?"

"No, in Rome. She's studying music there. She told me she didn't come to her mother's funeral because she knew it would be chock-a-block with celebrities who wouldn't know her and whom she didn't want to meet. And anyway, she doesn't like funerals. To tell the truth, I thought it sounded as if she didn't like her mother much. But she seemed very glad to be asked to come here and she agreed with me that the family quarrel was all nonsense and ought to be forgotten. And I believe the idea that she might make her home with us, at least for a time, really attracted her."

"You actually suggested that to her, did you?" I said. "Hubert's given in about it?"

"Yes, of course, as I knew he would. He always does in the end, you know." She laughed as she poured out a drink for herself and we both sat down. "When he knows I really want something badly he never holds out for long, bless him. He's such a kind old thing."

"When is she coming?"

"Not for two or three weeks. She's going to telephone when she's arranged things at her end, then I'm going to meet her at Heathrow. But I've made it quite plain to her that she needn't stay here a day longer than she wants to. She's got such a sweet voice, Virginia, and in only a few minutes I felt we were talking as if we'd known each other for years."

Perhaps it should not have done so, but it made me feel a curious depression. There was something unreal about it. Ann was building altogether too much on that few minutes' talk on the telephone. It seemed to me that this new relationship was dangerously important to her and that she might easily be in for some pain and shock if the girl of the sweet voice, who had already been in trouble with the police for possessing cannabis, did not turn out as she hoped.

I am not sure what I might have said, though probably it would not have been anything much, if Hubert and Felix had not come into the room at that moment.

They were looking very pleased with one another, so at least the first day had gone well.

"Well, we've made a beginning," Hubert said as he supplied Felix and himself with drinks, "though I realize it isn't going to be as simple a job as I somehow expected. I keep wandering from the point and your husband isn't as firm about it as I think he ought to be, Virginia. We've spent a good deal of today just chatting, and I can't help feeling he's the one who ought to be writing his autobiography, not me. I've always felt I've had a very interesting life, but I've been finding some of his stories fascinating. That time he spent with the Aborigines in Australia, for instance, when they saved his life in the desert when he was working on an irrigation scheme and got separated from his party, and they took his clothes so that he had to go naked, but they fed him for weeks. Remarkable."

It was no longer remarkable to me. It was one of Felix's favourite stories about himself, though the truth was that he had never set foot in Australia.

"And the way he broke his leg," Hubert went on, "trying to stop the fellow who was riding off after holding up a sub-post office. It helped the police to catch up with the chap."

Felix met my eyes with a look of bland innocence. He knew me well enough to feel secure that I would not give him away if I could help it, even to these close friends. We did not linger long over our drinks. It had struck me that he was looking unusually tired and that probably his leg was hurting more than he wanted to disclose. It was just like him to do his best to try to entertain his employer with his absurd fantasies, while saying nothing about something that was real and interesting.

I was right about the pain, because he took some pain-killers when we reached home, lit a cigarette, then lay down on the sofa, giving a sigh of relief at being able to relax. He even accepted another drink, which, as I have said, was unusual for him, because he always drank with great caution.

Gazing up at the ceiling, he observed, "The silly old coot. One wonders how someone so naïve could hold down a senior job in the Civil Service."

"Hubert? Because he swallowed your stories, d'you mean?" I put a match to the fire, which I had laid before we went out in the morning. "You do tell them rather convincingly, you know, at least to someone who isn't used to you."

"No, because the poor old bastard has the knack of making quite exciting stories sound just about as thrilling as the minutes of a committee meeting on drains. I realize that my job is going to be to put a little colour into his drivelling."

"That should come quite naturally to you. Only don't go too far. How do you actually work together?"

"Well, as he told you, today we didn't do much but chat, but it all went down on tape and tomorrow I'll have to get down to the job of editing it. He's going up to London to see a man about new locks for his doors and windows. Time he did it, too, I told him. A child could pick the locks they've got in that house. I like him, though. Better than that wife of his. She looks at me as if I were something that got washed up out of a sewer."

"I'm afraid that's because she thinks you done me wrong," I explained. "And that really isn't my fault. I've always said as little about you as possible."

"Which naturally led her to believe it was all far too terrible to talk about—which from my point of view it was. I was far more hurt than you ever understood. I've never really grasped what you had against me, and that's very painful in its way. What are we going to have to eat this evening?"

If Felix had not been crippled the probability was that he would have volunteered to cook our meal himself. As I have said, he was an excellent cook. But as things were, of course I had to do it. While I had been out earlier in the day I had bought two steaks, the makings of a salad, some cheese, and a bottle of our supermarket's undistinguished claret. When it was ready I put it on a tray and put the tray down on the coffee table beside the sofa. Felix was looking too worn for me to expect him to drag himself to the dining table. We ate by the fireside in a quiet mood that felt unexpectedly companionable and really very pleasant.

Next morning I drove Felix to the Brightwells again, then picked him up in the evening. And so it went on for the next few days. We slipped easily into a routine. He assured me that the work was going well. His job was to edit what Hubert recorded on tape, then discuss the results with him, and so far Hubert seemed satisfied. At times he appeared to be a little fractious at the improvements which Felix saw fit to make in his work, but Hubert was a modest man and ready to believe that Felix, the expert, knew best.

I had a feeling that this satisfactory situation might not last long and that sooner or later Hubert would realize that Felix knew no more about writing an autobiography than he did himself, but at least for the present it not only brought Felix in a certain amount of money but also gave him something to occupy him while his leg was mending.

I was surprised at how much I enjoyed his company. It no longer felt painful to find myself laughing at some of the more fantastic stories he told me about himself, because I knew quite well that at the back of his mind that was what he expected, perhaps even wanted me to do. Was that how he had always felt, I wondered. Had he really been distressed when I caught him out in some lie, or had he never intended that I should believe him? Had I always taken him too seriously?

Now, if I started laughing at something that he had told me, he often started laughing too, though perhaps a little uneasily, as if he was not quite certain what the joke was, though he was ready to share it. We usually played chess in the evenings, at which we were about evenly matched, which is the main thing necessary to make the game enjoyable. However unskillful you are, if your opponent is equally so you can pass the time together reasonably agreeably.

One evening when I was driving him home from the Brightwells he mentioned that men from a London firm had been in the house all day, fitting the new locks that Hubert had ordered. Felix also told me something which I thought a good deal more important. The day had been fixed for Holly Noble's arrival from Rome. It was to be on the following Thursday and Ann was driving to Heathrow to meet her. They were to recognize each other by each wearing a small artificial white rose on her lapel.

"I'd like to know what the girl's really expecting to get out of it," Felix said. "D'you think it's money? You'd think her mother must have left her a good deal, but you never know with these show business types. Some of them seem to think they'll never get old and ill and live right up to and over their incomes."

"You don't think Holly's just attracted by what Ann's offering her?" I said. "A home and some security and stability. And perhaps, if she's lucky, some affection too."

"Well, do you?" He sounded sceptical.

"I don't think it's altogether impossible. Do you know how old she is?"

"I think she's seventeen."

"Isn't that a bit young to be cast adrift alone in the world?"

"You don't know much about the modern young. I shouldn't think she'll be alone for long."

"So you think she might have some ulterior motive for coming to the Brightwells."

"That seems clear as day to me. And I just hate to think of how Ann's going to feel when she finds it out. She's invested an appalling amount of emotion in the situation. People really shouldn't do that when they haven't the least idea what they're letting themselves in for."

I had noticed that during the last day or two Felix and the Brightwells had progressed to Christian names, which indicated, I supposed, that Ann had come round to the view that Felix was human. His charm had worked as usual.

"By the way," he went on, "I believe you've met a character called Clyde Crendon."

"Yes, he was at lunch with the Brightwells on the day you came down here," I said. "Why?"

"He came over today to ask them to lunch with him next Sunday, but they told him they couldn't fix up anything till Holly got here. Then when he discovered I was your husband he invited you and me instead and I accepted. Is that all right?"

"I suppose so."

"What d'you make of him?"

"I liked him. And I've been meaning to get one of his books to see if they're as awful as people say."

"You shouldn't read the books of people you like, any more than you should meet people who've written books you've admired. You're probably in for disillusionment either way. But I've met him once before. It was a good while ago, before he'd had his great success. I think he was an Income Tax Inspector, or something like that. Nothing at all exciting."

It is not necessarily a recommendation to have been met by Felix. He is warm but indiscriminate in his friendships. I know of at least one burglar and one canon of St. Paul's, both of whom are friends of his. Anyone who shows some sign of liking him is accepted by him. And he is very loyal to his friends, after his fashion. For instance, he would never steal their little treasures, even when they attract him very much, and if they lend him money and he forgets to return it, it is no more than he would do for them if they happened to apply to him when he had something to spare. I really believe he has some moral standards, though I have never been able to discover just what they are.

It was in the evening of the following Thursday, when I went to the Brightwells' house to pick up Felix, that I was pressed eagerly by Ann to come in and meet Holly.

She had arrived from Rome that day and Ann had met her at Heathrow and driven her home. They had not been long in the house when I arrived. Holly's two suitcases were still in the hall, together with a violin case and with a fur jacket tossed down on top of them. Santos was just about to carry them upstairs. But I had time before he did so to notice that the cases were good and that the jacket was of mink. So it looked to me as if Felix's guess that Holly had come to the Brightwells to see what she could get out of them was probably mistaken.

On meeting her I thought that my own guess that she had come in the hope of finding a home, security, and stability, was much more likely to be right. She was a shy-looking girl, not very tall, slender and dark-haired. She seemed a bit lost, standing near the fireplace with a glass of sherry in her hand and with a gaze that met mine warily, almost as if I might constitute some danger to her.

But then she decided to risk a smile and it was a singularly sweet and friendly one. She was, I thought, nice-looking, though she had none of her mother's beauty. But some skilled Italian hairdresser had cropped her hair close to her well-shaped head, her small, rather sallow face was very slightly but very well made up, and the dark brown suit that she was wearing gave her slim figure distinction.

Tim and Barbie were there as well as Ann, Hubert, and Felix, and I did not wonder that the girl should look rather overpowered by finding herself among so many newfound relations and friends.

I asked her how long she had been in Rome and she answered, "Only six months." Her voice was low and husky and struck me as being theatrical. I wondered if her mother had taught her how to speak. "And I shouldn't have stayed much longer," she went on, "even if Aunt Ann hadn't invited me to stay. I'm really not at all musical. And I've got my A levels and would like to go to a university."

Ann corrected her. "Ann. I'm not your aunt, we're cousins. Let's just be Ann and Hubert."

The charming smile appeared again on the girl's face.

"That's nice. And it's so nice being here. I could hardly believe it when you telephoned. It was just what I was longing for, I mean, somewhere to come to in England where I could stay while I got things for the future sorted out. I promise I won't be any trouble. And I'll look for somewhere else to go as soon as I can."

We had all sat down and Hubert brought me a drink. Felix, sitting in a corner of the room, was nursing one and looking oddly troubled. I wondered if Hubert had begun to find out that he knew as little about the problems of writing an autobiography as he did himself.

"We're so very happy to have you," Ann said and laid a hand for a moment on Holly's shoulder. They were sitting side by side on the sofa. "You must stay as long as you like. But why not go on with your music? You'll at least play for us, won't you? I'm not much of a pianist, but I think I could manage to accompany you."

Holly gave her head a slight shake. "I don't think I'll ever touch my fiddle again. It was awful, how bad at it I was. I was really ashamed of myself among so many talented people."

"But if your mother believed in you enough to arrange for you to have an expensive training," Ann said, "I'm sure you must have some real talent of your own."

"She didn't believe in me," Holly said. "That isn't why she sent me to Rome. She just wanted me out of the way. I was old enough to have become a bit of an embarrassment to her. I think I was an embarrassment from the day I was born. I don't mean to say anything unkind about her now she's dead, because in her way she did her best for me. I mean, she sent me to a good school and away on all sorts of expensive holidays. But she didn't want me around. And my father was the same. He used to take me out occasionally, but he was married and had other children and he didn't want them to know I existed." She paused. "Perhaps I oughtn't to be talking like this, but I want to be sure you know how it was."

❊ ❊ ❊

Hubert looked confused. I could see he did not know how to react to such a speech. It sounded rehearsed to me, as if the girl had made up her mind that her relations should be told the facts about her illegitimate birth as soon as possible.

He muttered, "Quite—just so," without seeming to know what he meant by it.

Ann exclaimed, "But, darling, no one cares about that sort of thing anymore. Of course we're sorry about it, because it sounds as if you never had a real home before. But at least you can be sure you're very welcome here."

"You're so good," Holly said softly. "I wish I'd met you long ago."

I could not think why Felix was frowning in the way that he was. His gaze was abstracted. Suddenly looking at me, he said abruptly, "Isn't it time we were going, Virginia?"

Picking up his crutches, he began to get to his feet.

"Oh, must you go?" Ann said, but she said it absently. For the moment her attention was entirely occupied by the girl beside her. "We'll be seeing you on Sunday at Clyde Crendon's, shan't we, Virginia? We didn't accept his invitation till we found out if Holly would like to go out so soon after getting here, and there was her mother's death too—we didn't know if she'd prefer not to meet strangers for the time being. But she knows his books and says she'll be thrilled to meet him."

"Oh yes!" Holly exclaimed, her face lighting up. "It'll be fantastic."

Of course she did not mean that it would be in the least fantastic in the sense that I should have meant if I had used the word. She did not mean that there would be anything strange, fanciful, dreamlike in meeting the plump little man, but merely that it would be very nice. It is odd how rapidly fashion changes in words that express approval. Fantastic will soon be gone, along with super and smashing and ripping before it.

I finished my drink and stood up.

"Yes, we'll see you then," I said and went out with Felix, who seemed to be more in a hurry to get away than he usually is from even the smallest of parties.

He was silent on the way home. I asked him if something was wrong, but he did not answer. I did not press him. It would have been a waste of effort, because when he is in the kind of mood that he appeared to be in just then, withdrawn and perhaps sullen about something or other, it is useless to try to find out why he is brooding.

When we reached home he went as usual to the sofa, stretched himself out on it and lit a cigarette, while I lit the fire, then went out to the kitchen to put a small joint of lamb that I had bought in my lunch hour into the oven and peel some potatoes to go round it. When that was done I returned to the sitting room.

At first I thought that he was going to remain silent, still pondering something that had upset him, but as I sat down by the fire he spoke suddenly.

"Virginia, how much do those people mean to you?"

"The Brightwells?" I said.

"Yes."

"Well, they're friends."

"Are they important to you?"

"What do you mean by important? We've known each other for several years. They've always been very nice to me. I like them."

"And that's all?"

"Isn't that quite a lot? Sometimes one hardly likes one's friends at all. One just sticks to them out of habit and because we at least know the worst about one another."

"I see."

"I don't," I said. "What's worrying you? Is it something to do with the job?"

"Oh no, that's going pretty well."

"Then it's got something to do with that girl."

He did not answer, but only reached for another cigarette and lit it.

I had been getting used to the smell of tobacco smoke in the house, but all of a sudden I thought how much I disliked it and it made me irritable.

"You've taken against her, haven't you?" I said. "Why? Have you met her before?"

"Oh no," he said, but so quickly that I immediately became convinced that he must have done so.

"What d'you know about her?" I asked. "I know she's been in trouble with the police about drugs, but the Brightwells know all about that. But is there anything else?"

"I don't know anything about her," he answered. "Not a damned thing, except…"

"Well?" I said as he came to a full stop.

"No," he said after a moment. "Nothing. It's the drugs I was thinking about, but as the Brightwells know about them, that's all right, isn't it?"

Of course he was lying. He did know something about the girl, had perhaps even met her, though she had given no sign of recognizing him while I had been in the room, and since, as I have said, some of the people he mixes with are, to put it mildly, dubious, I grew very uneasy as well as irritable.

But if one has anything to do with Felix one has to accept him as he is. So I said nothing more about the matter. I have never felt any inclination to knock my head against brick walls.

# Chapter Three

I bought one of Clyde Crendon's paperbacks next day, as I felt that it would be only courteous to have read something that he had written before I went to have lunch with him on Sunday.

I found that it was not as full of sex and sadism as I had been led to believe. That is to say, the one chapter with a fair amount of both of them in it was so laboured and artificial that I felt it did not come from his heart at all. There was a good deal of blood in it, and broken bones and spilled brains, but I could not help feeling that it had been inserted into the story purely for the sake of the sales. And the sex hardly moved me, because it was quite unlike anything that I had ever experienced myself. But the man could tell a story. There was no doubt about that. Just what that quality is I cannot say, but I took the book with me to read in bed and did not turn the light out until I had finished it a little after one o'clock, which is much later than my usual time for going to sleep.

On Sunday Felix and I, the Brightwells with Holly, and Tim and Barbie all met at his house. The day was bright and mild, with the sweet sense of spring stirring in the air. The house had probably been built in the seventeenth century and once been two cottages and had had a thatched roof. But the thatch had been replaced by tiles, which must have been done a fair time ago because they were well weathered to a soft, mellow red. Inside the house what had once been two very small parlours had been thrown into one long room with a low, beamed ceiling and a big open fireplace at one end, in which a log fire was blazing.

Clyde Crendon, being short, was quite at ease in the room, but Tim and Hubert, both of whom were tall, each gave his head a good bump against a beam before learning to be cautious in the way he moved about. The furniture in the room was all modern and light-coloured, which I found pleasanter than anything sombrely in period would have been, and there was only one picture in the room, a portrait of a strange, green-eyed, long-necked woman, which I began by assuming was a print, then realized with a slight shock was an original Modigliani. It reminded me that unpretentious as the small house might be, the man whose book had kept me awake till one o'clock the night before must be very wealthy.

He was a fussy host, eagerly bestowing drinks on us, worrying about whether or not we were warm enough and were seated comfortably. Then he shepherded us into his dining room, where the housekeeper whom Ann had found for him provided an excellent meal of avocados, grilled sole, and caramel of oranges. The *Mâcon blanc* that went with it was agreeable. The coffee and the brandy afterwards were good. But Clyde Crendon himself bobbed up and down in his chair so often, refilling our glasses or pressing us to have second helpings of everything on the table, that I began to feel that however wealthy he might be, he was an anxious and inexperienced host. Perhaps, I thought, he was naturally a solitary man, not at all used to even this modest kind of entertaining, and who liked best to spend most of his time in his highly profitable daydreams.

After lunch he took us all round his garden, except for Felix, who said that if he might be excused he would prefer to sit by the fire and rest his leg. The garden was a mass of matted weeds, old roses that had not been pruned for years, and overgrown shrubs. Here and there a clump of daffodils bloomed boldly in the tangle.

Clyde Crendon asked Hubert for his advice as to how he should begin to tackle this disorder and Hubert said without hesitation that the first obvious step was to acquire a gardener, as things had been allowed to go so far that Clyde Crendon would not be able to cope with them alone unless he was ready to give all his time to it.

The previous owner, he told us, had been a woman who had lived in the house until she was ninety-one and had refused to have help of any kind. He had already had a good deal done to the house, installing central heating and a new kitchen and bathroom as well as having it completely redecorated. But was it possible to obtain a gardener, he asked. He thought that such people were very hard to come by. Ann said that she knew a man who she thought might be persuaded to take on the work. Ann always knew all that there was to know about such things.

We all wandered on along what had once been a path, with Clyde Crendon and Holly now leading the way. He was talking to her vivaciously, though she in her shy way was answering very little. I thought he was attracted by her, yet presently, when we reached what had once been a summerhouse and was now a ruin, overgrown with ivy, I suddenly realized that she was no longer with us. As we went into the summerhouse, tearing down cobwebs and disturbing wood lice, she had slipped away.

I thought I knew where she had gone and I turned out to be right. When we returned to the house we found her in the sitting room, talking to Felix. But he did not look as if this had given him any pleasure, though the girl was smiling, as if something had satisfied her. With a curious touch of irony in her voice, which did not suit her, she remarked that she had thought that someone ought to come back to cheer up the invalid, and Ann, who did not seem to notice the irony, murmured to me that she was such a nice girl, so kind and considerate.

But at that moment I saw something on Clyde Crendon's face that took me by surprise. Looking at Holly there was the watchfulness, the thoughtfulness that I had noticed in his eyes the first time I had met him. If he was attracted by her, as I had thought at first, it seemed to me that he was having doubts.

When the party broke up and I was driving Felix home I made another attempt to persuade him to talk about Holly.

"Felix, you do know that girl, or something about her," I said. "Why won't you tell me what it is?"

"All right," he said, "I'll tell you. I've met her. I met her once in the Fox and Grapes—that's that pub I expect you remember just round the corner from my place—but it was only for a few minutes. And that's absolutely all, except that she was with a man I happen not to like. And this afternoon, when she came in from the garden, she was asking me not to say anything about it to the Brightwells. She didn't recognize me the first time we met, but today for some reason she remembered me and she told me she wants so badly to make them like her, because this is such a wonderful chance for her to make a new start, and all that sort of thing, that she'd be everlastingly grateful if I didn't talk about having known the man I saw her with."

"Then is he very notorious?"

"Quite fairly."

"And are you going to say nothing?"

"I promised I wouldn't."

"Why did you do that?"

"Because I'm a weak-kneed character who thinks that just possibly she does want to make a new start. You remember I asked you how much the Brightwells mean to you. If you'd said they were very important to you perhaps I'd have acted differently."

"And that's really all you've got against her, that you saw her with that man?"

"Yes."

But he hesitated slightly before he said it and I knew that there was something more. But whatever it was, he had probably promised the girl that he would say nothing about it, and he is fairly faithful to his promises.

I began to wonder what I ought to do myself. Ought I to say anything to Ann to warn her that Holly might not be all that she appeared to be? I did not think that it would be much use. For the present Ann was infatuated, and after all, what evidence had I that anything was wrong? Merely the fact that Felix, who was not the most reliable of witnesses, claimed that he and she had met once in a pub called the Fox and Grapes, and that was hardly a criminal offence.

By chance I met Clyde Crendon a day or two later in the town. It was one of my days off and I had been doing some shopping. He asked me to have a drink with him and we went together into the Rose and Crown, an old pub that had become very sophisticated in recent times, that overlooked the market square. At first I thought that he was merely in a friendly mood and had no special reason for his invitation, but after a little while he asked me a disturbing question.

"Virginia, what is Felix really doing here?"

"What do you mean?" I asked. Nearly always a foolish question. It too obviously shows that one wants time to think.

"You know what I mean, don't you?" he said. "The job he's taken on for Brightwell—he hasn't the faintest idea how to go about it. I've seen him once or twice and talked to him a little about it and it's obvious he's never done anything of the kind before. So what's he really doing here?"

"Trying to earn a little money when the chance came his way," I said, "and fill the time in till his leg's mended. What else should he be doing?"

"I don't know, but I've been wondering if there was anything else behind it."

"What, for instance?"

He shrugged his shoulders, showing that he had nothing special to suggest.

"It's just that I'm a professional and I can spot an amateur," he said. "The odd things he says about it—they don't ring true.

And it's obvious he hates it when I try to talk about it in a friendly way. Of course, we all start as amateurs, not knowing what it may be going to turn us into when we've stuck to it for a time, but I don't think he's even interested in the work. And what's more, I think Brightwell's spotted it. If Felix doesn't try to do better, he'll lose his job."

"Well, thank you for warning me," I said. "I'll tell him, shall I?"

"If you think you should."

I took a long look at his round, rosy face.

"Clyde, what have you really got on your mind?"

He gave an embarrassed smile.

"Nothing—nothing at all."

"You haven't got it into your head he's going to make off with something valuable, have you, like, say, a Baraud painting? To be honest with you, Felix is a bit of a thief, but he never takes anything too large to slip into a pocket."

He assumed I was mocking him, rather than speaking the literal truth. He flushed.

"I'm sorry I ever said anything about it," he said. "I just thought I might be able to help. I mean, by telling you that Brightwell's getting dissatisfied. It worries me that Felix and that girl Holly certainly know one another and seem to want to pretend they don't. But I suppose you know all about that."

I thought how observant of him it had been to spot that Holly and Felix knew one another. That penetrating gaze of his was on me now and I wondered what he was thinking.

"You sound as if you don't like her much," I said, remembering that I had thought in his garden that he was attracted by her.

"I've nothing against her," he said. "But I think in her own way she's very tough. Probably she's had to be, living in the shadow of her mother. It was that or go under. But I don't think Lady Brightwell has understood that and I think she's got hopes and is making plans for the girl that will come to nothing. It worries me, because I like Lady Brightwell very much."

It worried me too. But only that evening I discovered that I had underrated Ann and that she understood far more than I had given her credit for. When I went as usual to collect Felix she asked me in for a drink and almost as soon as we were settled by the fire, she said abruptly, "Virginia, Holly isn't happy here. What do you think I ought to do about it?"

"Where is she now?" I asked.

"I think she's gone to the cinema, or perhaps to have her hair done," Ann answered. "I'm not sure. She doesn't like it if I ask her what she means to do. You wouldn't think it to look at her, but she can snap back quite hard if she thinks you're interfering with her. And I don't mean to interfere, I only want to show her that I take an interest in her and care about her. But I don't think she's ever had anyone care about her before and she thinks it means I'm trying to control her, and that's the last thing I want to do. She says she wants to go to a university to do Social Science and I've been trying to find out what steps she ought to take so that she can start somewhere or other in the autumn, but she seems to want me to leave everything entirely to her. Isn't it tragic to think of the kind of childhood she must have had to be so terribly on the defensive when all she's being offered is affection?"

"And you don't think she'll stay?"

Ann gave an unhappy shake of her head.

"I'm afraid not. Not much longer."

"Where will she go?"

"I don't know. She talks very little about her background. She doesn't talk about her school, or any friends she made there, or where she used to spend her holidays. She talks a good deal about her mother, but simply as an artist, not as a human being."

"Perhaps she wasn't very human."

"I don't think she can have been."

The door opened and Hubert and Felix came in. Both had somewhat grim looks on their faces and I wondered if they had had a disagreement.

"Ah, there you are," Ann said. "I was just telling Virginia that I don't think Holly's going to stay with us much longer."

"Won't worry me if she doesn't," Hubert grunted.

"Don't you like her?" I asked.

"I've never much use for the young," he answered. "Too self-satisfied. Too sure the world revolves around them. I think we were much more comfortable before she came. But Ann likes having her, so I'll put up with it as long as I must. But I'm about tired of hearing from her how wonderful that mother of hers was as Lady Macbeth with that chap Cairns. He's one of the actors I can't stand. I watched him on television the other evening. He bellows. I don't pretend to know much about Shakespeare, but I do know he oughtn't to be bellowed."

Felix was offered a drink but declined it, and soon afterwards we left, after Ann had asked me once more what I thought she might do to induce Holly to stay.

I had no advice to give her. If, as she thought, the girl was unhappy, then it seemed to me that the sooner she left the better, before Ann had formed too great a dependence on her. On the other hand, if she was simply the kind of adolescent who for a time is unhappy wherever she goes and needs time to grow out of this state of mind, then it seemed possible that in the end Ann's affection might gradually come to mean something to her and might help the girl through that difficult period of her life. To think that it had done so would give great happiness to Ann.

On the way home I told Felix about my talk with Clyde Crendon.

"He's rumbled you," I said. "He knows you don't know anything about what you're doing. And he thinks Hubert has begun to realize it too and that if you want to keep the job you'll have to put more of an effort into it."

"The trouble is, it bores me," Felix said.

"It isn't just that you've discovered with horror that it's a little too like hard work?"

"It *is* hard work," he admitted. "A good deal harder than I expected. That's Hubert's fault. I don't know how he got it into his head that he was capable of writing an autobiography, but I'm having to scrap almost everything he puts on tape and work it up from scratch. And I'm not even sure he cares much about the result. He's just reliving the exciting days of his youth and having a wonderful time with me as a captive audience. You may find it difficult to believe now, but he was a murderous bastard. Of course he was a hero, and I know we all owe an immense amount to people like him, but when he was a commando he really enjoyed stalking some unsuspecting chap in the dark and slitting his throat. And that slightly makes my flesh creep."

"You don't think you'd have done it yourself if you'd been a bit over one year old in those days?"

"Virginia, you know me," he said. "I'm a complete coward. I'd have looked for a nice safe job with the ground staff of the R.A.F., or something like that."

I have never had any opportunity to check how much courage Felix has. I imagine that like most people there are some forms of terror that he could face and others that he could not. I suppose we are fortunate that neither he nor I have ever been seriously tested.

"Anyway, you won't mind it much if the job comes to an end," I said.

"Suppose it does," he said, "can I stay here till I can get around a bit better? I'm not being too much of a nuisance, am I?"

He was being hardly any nuisance at all. What was worrying me most about having him to live with me was that I was enjoying it a little too much. Six years ago, when I had made up my mind to leave him because I found that I could not stand the strain of living with someone who was nothing but a petty crook, it had been so painful that I was quite alarmed by the thought of having to go through something of the same sort again.

I did not answer and he did not repeat the question. He probably realized that I did not mean to commit myself, even if he knew that it was unlikely that I would turn him out to fend for himself in his maimed condition.

I said, "Clyde seemed to think you might have some sinister reason for being here."

"He really said that, did he?" Felix asked.

"Not exactly, but he kept asking me what you were really doing, since it was obvious you weren't an experienced ghostwriter."

"The man's a fool." But he said it indifferently, as if the opinions of Clyde Crendon were of no importance to him. "What does worry me somewhat is that if I make too much of a mess of the job I'll be letting Tim down. He persuaded Hubert to take me on because he knew I was looking for something to do, and it would be a pity to get Tim in bad with the Brightwells. I think he's got what are called expectations from them."

"If he has, he's going to have to wait a long time for them to come to anything," I said. "Hubert's probably good for another twenty years and Ann for more than that."

"But I think they're quite generous to him now. I know they bought him and Barbie that cottage they've got down here, and Tim's always talked as if it's important for him to keep on the right side of them."

"And I thought he was just fond of them. But it's mainly mercenary, is it?"

"Oh, I wouldn't say that. I think he's very fond of them. But now that I know more about Hubert than I did, I see it wouldn't be too difficult to get across him. For instance, he and I had quite a quarrel today merely because I told him he'd been repeating himself. I could prove it in black and white that he had, but that didn't go down at all well."

"I thought something was wrong when you came into the drawing room together," I said. "That's all it was, was it?"

"Absolutely all," he said with such conviction that I immediately felt that he and Hubert must have had some other, more serious cause of disagreement.

That turned out to be the case. After a moment Felix chuckled and said, "I may as well tell you what really happened, because in its way it was quite funny. I was in his study, you see, waiting for him, and I happened to pick up a rather striking sort of paper knife that was lying on his desk. And I was holding it, making passes in the air, pretending I was stabbing someone in the back with it, when he came in and roared at me to put it down. It seems the knife was something I ought never to have touched. It's the one that slit a lot of German throats and it's sort of sacred to him. He was really quite angry about it."

"I suppose you weren't just about to slip it into your pocket when he came in and caught you," I said.

"Oh come, you know I'd never touch anything belonging to him or Ann."

I was inclined to believe him. They were friends of mine, which with luck rendered them immune to his depredations.

### ❀ ❀ ❀

That evening I had a telephone call from Barbie. She and Tim were in London but she had rung up to invite Felix and me to have dinner with them at the Rose and Crown the next evening, as they were coming down to their cottage for the weekend, or perhaps for longer. Sometimes they stayed there for several weeks, driving up daily to the offices of *The Platform*. I arranged with her that we should meet them in the bar of the Rose and Crown at seven, and when I had picked Felix up as usual next day from the Brightwells' I drove straight to the old pub and we made our way to the bar.

We were early and Tim and Barbie had not arrived yet, so Felix ordered drinks for us and we sat down at a table in a corner.

There was no one else in the bar just then, but after a few minutes two men came in, perched on stools at the bar and ordered beer. I doubt if I should have paid any attention to them if I had not noticed at that moment a sudden concentration in Felix's gaze as he looked at them, as if he had just received a shock. It made me look at them too, but I could not see anything special about them.

They seemed to me two very ordinary men. And now Felix carefully averted his eyes from them and began to talk rapidly about what he would do when he was able to have the plaster removed from his leg and could get about normally.

He said that before his accident he had been planning to go to Canada, then to work his way southwards through the United States and into Mexico and that that was what he still hoped to be able to do in time.

Since some other people came in then and sat down at a table near us I imagine I should have taken no more notice of the two men sitting at the bar if they had not got up, moved to a table and sat down, and as they did so had suddenly seen Felix.

When that happened I saw the same sort of concentration come into their eyes as I had seen in Felix's. They then exchanged looks for a moment and seemed to be at a loss. I thought that one of them was in his late thirties, the other in his twenties. The older man was big, with heavy shoulders, a thick neck, coarse features, and badly shaven cheeks. He was wearing a pullover with a high roll collar and a cheap brown suit that looked too tight to cover his bulging muscles. The younger was a small, sharp-featured man with upstanding fair hair, small grey eyes with hardly any lashes, so that they had a peculiarly naked look, and noticeably long, bony hands which he kept restlessly on the move, tugging at an ear, scratching his chest, clawing through his hair. He was wearing jeans and a black plastic jacket.

Now that I was looking at the two of them more carefully than I had at first, I thought that they did not look altogether ordinary. They looked like people whom I should not care to encounter alone on a dark night. However, Felix was still ignoring them and after their first startled glance at him they ignored him. But they finished their drinks quickly and left. It seemed to me that once they had gone Felix relaxed.

"Did you know those two men?" I asked.

I should have known better than to do that, because of course he said that he did not. But I went on, "I'd an impression they knew you."

"Here are Tim and Barbie," he said.

They had just come into the bar. Barbie was in one of her well-cut tweed suits and shoes as usual with very high heels, which she stuck to even in their country cottage. Tim was in slacks and a suede jacket. Neither of them looked as if Allingford was really the right place for them, but then they never did. Apparently it had started to rain, for both had a slight sprinkling of raindrops on their hair.

After joining us at our table, Tim went to the bar and ordered gin and tonic for them both and we sat and chatted for a time, mostly about how Felix was getting along with Hubert and his autobiography. Felix stated that it was going very well and that though it was sometimes heavy going, trying to keep Hubert to the point, he found the work very interesting. Tim said he was glad to hear it, but his smile was sceptical and he added that he could not imagine his uncle having anything to say about his life that would not be boring in the extreme.

"They're an intriguing contrast, aren't they, my uncle and Clyde Crendon?" he said. "I don't suppose Crendon's been within smelling distance of any of the violence he writes about, yet writing about it has made him a really rich man. And my uncle's been through hell and horror and been a real hero and got a string of decorations and I don't suppose for a moment he'll get his autobiography published."

"That'll be up to Felix," Barbie said. "It's what he's here for."

"Well, I'm doing my best, but I've some doubts about it myself," Felix said. "Will it be a very bitter blow for him if everyone turns it down?"

"A blow to his pride, naturally," Tim said. "But luckily it won't mean anything financially. He and Ann have a good deal of money apart from his pension. And now they've discovered how valuable those Baraud paintings are, they can always cash in on those. To tell the truth, I wish they would. It's tempting providence to have anything like them in the house."

"Or if not providence, some common or garden art thieves," Barbie said. "I wonder how many people know about them."

"Plenty," Tim said. "Ann's always showed them off when she could, even before his prices rocketed. Only the other day a man who does some work for *The Platform* and who runs a gallery asked me if there was any chance she'd consider selling. I told him I was sure there wasn't for the present. How she'll feel about it if the prices go higher still, which it seems quite likely they will, I don't know. Suppose it struck her one day it might be nice to have a Rolls, for instance, and a yacht, and perhaps a nice old Georgian mansion somewhere, and a staff of servants. In other words, to live the life of the really rich. If once it occurred to her, you know, I think she might find she didn't mind parting with the Barauds. Who would?"

"I should," Barbie said. "I don't want a Rolls, or a yacht, or a mansion, or a staff of servants. All I want is not actually to have to worry about money. I like our cottage and our flat and I like my job and our way of living. And d'you realize that if one suddenly became enormously rich one would probably lose most of one's friends? They'd feel they couldn't keep up with one."

"That's because temptation's never come your way," Tim said. "You're sensible and keep your daydreams reasonably realistic. So do I. All the same, I shouldn't mind being rich. Very, very rich…"

They smiled at one another as if this were a private joke. I had noticed before that they were fond of having private jokes, as they had had when they knew I was going to find Felix waiting for me in my home, prepared to pretend that he could help Hubert to write his autobiography.

"Personally I'd settle for a few hundred thousand," Felix said. "One could do very comfortably on that. But I agree with you, Tim, I think Ann and Hubert would be wise to get rid of the Barauds. It isn't nice being burgled. I've seen the results of it once or twice, and even if it's been done by professionals who've made a fairly clean job of it and not by some lunatic vandals, it's a sort of desecration of one's private life."

He sounded unexpectedly serious and his gaze strayed to the door of the bar, almost as if he thought that the two men who had come in and gone out again so hurriedly when they saw him might reappear.

That, at least, was what I thought he might be thinking about, though of course it might easily have been something quite different.

Later in the evening, after we had reached home, driving through what had become heavy rain, I questioned him about the two men. We had had a pleasant dinner with Tim and Barbie, all of us talking a good deal of nonsense about how unfortunate it would be to become really rich. What such a thing would do to me I did not know, but I had always had a belief that it would be the saving of Felix. If only he would fall in love with a woman who had a great deal of money and he and I arranged an amiable divorce, I believed he might find life so comfortable that he would take the trouble to go straight in order to preserve it.

But one of the reasons why this scheme of mine had never borne fruit was that he was not at all mercenary. When he fell in love with a woman, as he did from time to time, it was quite likely to be with someone whose very poverty had moved him to sympathy with her in her difficulties.

"About those men in the Rose and Crown," I said as we were drinking tea before going to bed, "you never told me if they know you."

He took so long to answer that I thought he did not mean to answer at all. But at last he said, "They may have thought they did."

"That means that you know them."

"I can't swear to it. I thought I did, but I'm not sure."

"Who are they?"

"Oh, I don't know their names."

"Then what do you know about them?"

"I told you, I'm not sure. I don't think I ever saw the big chap before, but I think the small one is someone I've met in the Fox and Grapes and had a chat with about who was likely to win the two-thirty. Not one of my interests, as you know, but it seemed to be the only thing he was inclined to talk about. And I heard he had a brother who was doing five years for breaking and entering and who was expected out soon. So perhaps that's who the big chap is."

"You mean they're a couple of burglars," I said.

"That's a possibility."

"For God's sake, Felix, say what you mean!" I exclaimed. "Are they burglars?"

He gave a reluctant nod. "At any rate, in their spare time. I don't know if they've got legitimate jobs too."

"Then what are they doing in Allingford?"

"I'm sure you've had the same thought about that as I have," he said.

"That they've come after the Barauds?"

"On the other hand, perhaps they're here just for a quiet weekend, like Tim and Barbie. It may be pleasant when you come out of gaol to have a peaceful rest in the country, away from all your old associates who got you into trouble. Alternatively, they maybe thinking of robbing a bank, or stealing the jewels of one of your wealthier residents. You and I happen to have the Barauds on our minds, but I can't really see those two as art thieves. They wouldn't know where to begin."

"All the same, they're burglars?"

"Yes."

"And the Barauds would be worth stealing, if someone had put them up to it."

"Unquestionably."

"Then oughtn't we to warn the Brightwells about it?"

He stirred restlessly on the sofa where he had taken up his usual place, with his leg in its plaster stretched out along it.

"Perhaps we should, though I'm not sure what good it would do," he said. "Do you expect Hubert to stand on guard with a shotgun, perhaps for days, till those two got round to doing the job? Or perhaps he might lurk in hiding with his paper knife, ready to strike. I suppose, come to think of it, he might rather enjoy that. But the fact is, he's already taken all the sensible precautions he can against being robbed. He's had new locks fixed on all the doors and windows and he's raised the insurance on the pictures. I'll warn him about these men, if you like, though I think it might be kinder to leave him and Ann in peace."

"He could get in touch with the police about them," I said, "and get them to keep the men under observation."

"That's true." But he did not look enthusiastic about my suggestion. "I can't say I like the idea of letting the Brightwells know too much about the company I keep. They might not understand it comes simply from my deep interest in human nature and that a study of men like the two we saw in the pub can be as absorbing as that of people like themselves. *Nostalgie de la boue*, perhaps. But what's wrong with that?"

"Felix, you just enjoy going into the Fox and Grapes and you don't mind whom you talk to when you get there," I said. "There's no need to get pompous about it. The fact remains that I think you should tell the Brightwells that you've seen these men, then they can tell the police about it or not, as they choose."

"All right," Felix said, but so indifferently that I did not feel sure that he meant it.

But if he did not, there was nothing to stop me doing it myself, I thought, so I did not pursue the matter. However, when I picked him up from the Brightwells' house the next evening, he told me that he had informed Hubert of the presence in Allingford of the two men whom we had seen in the Rose and Crown, and had even suggested to him that he should tell the police that they were in the neighbourhood. Even if the men had no interest in the Barauds, so Felix claimed that he had said, it might be useful to the police to know that they were here, possibly with some nefarious plot in mind. He did not know what Hubert was going to do about it.

"But you realize, we can't even be sure that they're staying in Allingford," he said. "They may just have dropped into the Rose and Crown for a drink on their way to do some other job. In fact, that seems to me quite likely."

"But they didn't like it when they saw you there."

"There are lots of people who might not be glad to see me all of a sudden. I'm not universally beloved."

"Oh, you know what I mean."

"I suppose I do. But I've done all I can about it, haven't I? Hubert can go to the police about it or not, as he chooses. It isn't my business."

"You don't think perhaps you ought to go to the police yourself?"

"No, that I certainly will not do," he said with some violence. "Have you forgotten the sacred principle of British law that people are innocent till they're proved guilty? All I could say for sure these men are guilty of is having a drink yesterday in a pub where you and I happened to be. No, Virginia, I'll do a lot to please you, particularly as you're being so good to me, but there are limits beyond which I will not go."

He was right, I supposed. I delivered him at the front door of the house, then drove the car into the garage.

As I followed Felix into the house I heard the telephone ringing. He had already settled himself on the sofa and made no effort to get up and answer it. I hurried towards it, but a moment before I reached it, it stopped.

"Never mind," he said. "If it's important they'll ring again presently."

That might be true, but I was left with the sense of anxious frustration that comes to me whenever I have failed to reach a telephone in time to answer a call. Just that call, I always think, that call of all others that I have missed simply because I was out of the house, might be the most important call that had ever been made to me in my life.

Trying to be rational about it is not much use. I was impatient and on edge as I went out to the kitchen and started preparing the chicken that I was going to roast. It was seven o'clock and the chicken was nearly cooked before the telephone rang again.

I pounced on it as if I were afraid that it might try to escape me. To say that I had a premonition that the call was important would be absurd, because I often have such premonitions and then forget all but the few occasions when it turns out that I have been right. But I had one of those premonitions then, I suppose because of the impatient way that I had been waiting for the earlier call to be repeated. It was almost a disappointment when I heard Ann's voice. Calls from her were a normal part of my day.

"Virginia, I tried to call you before, but I suppose you hadn't got home yet," she said. There was something unusual about her voice. It was very level, but it sounded as if it were an effort for her to keep it so. "I suppose you haven't seen Holly?"

"No," I said.

"When did you see her last?" Ann asked.

It seemed a strange question.

"I'm not sure—yesterday morning, I think, when I delivered Felix."

"You haven't seen her today?"

"No." Then I woke up to the fact that something was seriously the matter. "What's wrong, Ann?" I asked. "Is she in trouble of some sort?"

"She's gone," Ann said.

"What d'you mean, gone?"

"Disappeared."

"But when?"

"Sometime today."

"You mean she's left you without telling you she was going?"

"Perhaps that's it, only she's left her violin and her mink jacket behind."

"Then she's probably coming back, isn't she? You've told me she doesn't like telling you what she means to do."

"But she went out soon after breakfast and she didn't come back for lunch and she still hasn't come back, and she's never done anything like that before. And I want you to tell me—one hears of such awful things that happen nowadays—d'you think I ought to tell the police about it? Hubert says I'm being stupid and that she's just in a funny mood and will walk in at any moment, but I can't help it, I'm so frightened. Virginia, I simply can't help believing she's been kidnapped!"

# Chapter Four

I said, "Oh no!" But I was not sure what I meant by it.

I remember the sound of the rain drumming against the windowpanes. It had been raining on and off all day. The beautiful spring weather that we had been having seemed to have absconded, leaving winter a chance to come back. To my imagination the rain against the windows had an alarmingly ominous sound.

Ann went on hurriedly, "But how else can you explain it? She goes out after breakfast, wearing a tweed suit and one of those quilted jackets everyone wears now, and leaving behind that lovely mink jacket she's got, and she hasn't come back yet. What can she have been doing all this time if she hasn't been— hasn't been stopped?"

"Do you know if she had a handbag with her?" I asked.

"I'm not sure," Ann answered. "I think so."

"Then she's probably got some money with her."

"I suppose so."

"So that if she just suddenly decided she'd like to go to London for some reason or other, she could have gone."

"But why should she do a thing like that?"

"God knows. But hasn't she been in trouble once for being in possession of drugs? Suppose that the feeling came on that she'd got to get hold of some again and she had to go to London to get it."

"Is that what you really think she's done?"

"I don't know what I think, Ann. It's just a suggestion."

"But you don't believe I could be right—I mean, that she's been kidnapped?"

"I don't know. I wish I could help, but I hardly know the girl. You and Hubert are much more likely to be able to guess what she'd do than I am."

"I told you, Hubert thinks I'm being stupid, and really you agree with him, don't you?"

"I'm not sure. You might be right that she's in trouble. Why don't you call the police in any case? It can't do any harm."

"But suppose they just think I'm bothering them about nothing."

"I can't see that it matters if they do. But I don't imagine they will."

I heard her give a long-drawn sigh. "You really think that's what I ought to do?"

"The only other thing you can do is wait and see," I said. "Perhaps you might wait a little longer. It depends how you feel about it yourself."

There was silence for a moment, then Ann went on, "If you're right that she went to London to get a supply of drugs, then I could get her into trouble by calling the police."

"Oh, that was just a wild guess of mine," I said. "I shouldn't take it seriously."

"I'd hate to get her into trouble."

"Then wait for a little while. But if she doesn't come home for the night, I'd certainly call the police."

"Yes, yes, I'm sure you're right. I'll tell Hubert what you said. I'll wait a bit longer and see what happens, then if she doesn't come home I'll let the police know I'm afraid she's been kidnapped. Or, you know—you know, it could be something worse, Virginia. I can hardly bring myself to think of it, but one hears of such awful things happening. Suppose she accepted a lift from someone, or something like that—No! No, I'm sure she wouldn't do that. She's quite sensible. She knows her way around. Oh God, I feel so helpless. I feel responsible for her, you see, and yet I don't know what to do. But thank you for your advice. I'll wait a bit longer, then call the police, even if they think I'm making a fuss about nothing. Good night."

She rang off.

"What was all that about?" Felix asked as I put the telephone down.

I told him, then went out to the kitchen to attend to the chicken.

We ate at the dining table, since Felix was now becoming relatively agile and no longer needed his meals on a tray by the fire. We were almost silent, for I was turning over in my mind what Ann had told me and wondering what the girl was really up to, and Felix also seemed to have private thoughts on which he was concentrating and which, to go by the look on his face, were disturbing.

I had cleared the table and stacked the dishwasher and made some coffee and brought it into the sitting room before he said suddenly, "I shouldn't be surprised if you're right."

"About what?" I asked.

"That the girl's gone up to London to stock up on dope. By now it may be something more serious than the cannabis, which was the trouble before. And my own feeling is that if she were to stay there instead of coming back to Allingford it would be better for the Brightwells."

"So you do know something about her," I said. "More than you've told me."

He did not answer, which I took to be an admission that I was right, though I realized that I would not be able to induce him to say so.

"But suppose I'm wrong about the drugs and Ann's right that she's been kidnapped," I said.

"Then there'll be a kidnap note in a day or two, won't there?"

"I wish I knew what you really think about it, Felix."

"Only that what you told Ann was perfectly sound. I mean, that she should wait a little longer, then notify the police that the girl's missing."

"Yes, but do you think that she's been kidnapped?"

"I don't know any more about it than you do. She may have been knocked down by a car and killed. Or she may be lying unidentified after an accident of some kind in a hospital. Or she may have lost her memory and gone wandering off God knows where. Or she may have been raped and murdered." He lit a cigarette. "For the moment there's no guessing what may have happened."

"Except that you do know something about her that might give a clue to it, and I think you ought to tell the Brightwells about it."

He frowned darkly, then shook his head.

"I can't very well do that," he said.

"Why not?"

"Because, little though it is, they'll want to know why I didn't tell them straightaway and that would put me in a rather awkward position."

"But if Holly's really gone missing, if she doesn't turn up in another hour or two, hadn't you better face that?"

He shook his head again. "Nothing that I could tell them would help. If they do get a kidnap note…"

"Well?" I said as he paused.

"I'll advise them not to pay it. As I told you, I think they'd be well rid of her."

"And you're going to tell them that, though you refuse to tell them why?"

"All right then, I'll say nothing at all about it. They aren't likely to ask me for my advice."

"Then I think I'll tell them that you know something and that you might be able to help the police in their inquiries."

"If you do that, I'll simply deny it."

"Mayn't they be able to trace a connection between the two of you?"

He inhaled deeply on his cigarette and breathed smoke out through his nostrils.

"No, there's no risk of that. Honestly, Virginia, there's no connection. I met her just the once, as I told you."

"And you didn't like the company she was in."

"Just so. That's absolutely all."

I gave up at that point. Whatever he was keeping to himself, he intended to keep it so.

However, in bed that night I turned over in my mind what I ought to do if Holly had not returned to the Brightwells' house that evening. Ought I to tell them that I was convinced that Felix knew something about her which might help to explain what had happened? It seemed to me fairly clear that I ought. Yet I had very little to go on and Felix was certain to deny the truth of anything I told them. All the same, would it not be best to tell them what I believed?

But one of my problems in my relationship with Felix has always been that I hate giving away to other people that statements that he has made are likely to be lies, or that he is planning to trick them in any way. Wives are not required to give evidence against their husbands in a court of law, and even if Felix was not exactly my husband anymore, the old tie had never been entirely broken. If I told Ann and Hubert that he had some knowledge of Holly and they told this to the police, might it not land him in serious trouble?

I slept badly, haunted by dreams which I knew on waking had been frightening, though I could not remember what they had been.

As soon as I had made coffee and drunk my first cup of it, I telephoned Ann and asked her if Holly had returned.

She sounded tearful. "No."

"And she hasn't telephoned or anything? You don't know anything about what's happened to her?"

"Nothing at all. I was just going to telephone the police when you rang. Even Hubert agrees now that I ought to do that. I thought I ought to do it yesterday evening, but he said it wasn't as if she was a child who couldn't go missing for more than an hour or two without something being wrong. But now he says we must do it. And oh, Virginia, I'm so scared in case they tell us almost at once that something awful's happened. I'd almost sooner not know. I know that's all wrong and very cowardly, but I can't help it."

"I'll be bringing Felix along in an hour or two," I said, "then you can let me know if they've been able to tell you anything."

"Yes," she said. "Yes, of course."

As I rang off I reflected that of all the things that might have happened to Holly since her disappearance, as Felix had listed them, my own suggestion that she had gone to London to stock up on drugs was actually by far the least horrifying.

When Felix and I arrived at the Brightwells' house that morning I went in with him instead of driving away as soon as he was out of the car, as I usually did, and when Ann came running to the door to meet us I asked her if she had any news yet of Holly.

"No," she said, "but we've told the police about it and they're sending someone out here to get the details. They seemed to think we'd done the right thing, letting them know. I'm glad we did it. But now that we have, Hubert's started muttering that she's only being troublesome. He's never taken to her, you know. He'd be glad if he never saw her again."

He had come out of his study into the hall and had heard what she had said.

"I can't say I wouldn't be glad if she left us," he said, "but in a proper manner, without all this melodrama that's got us actually calling in the police. It's true I've never taken to her. She's a strange girl and I wish she'd never come here. But I realize this disappearance of hers may not actually be her fault, so we've got to take steps about it. We've no choice. But if she does walk in sometime soon, as if she'd done nothing unusual and hadn't put us to any trouble, she's going to get some very straight talking from me."

"She won't come back," Ann said. "She's gone. I don't think we'll ever see her again."

I said then that I would keep in touch and left them.

I had a busy day ahead of me at the clinic and I had not much time to think about Holly, though from time to time I felt an urge to telephone Ann and ask if she had any information yet about the girl. But in the end I waited till the evening, when I was picking Felix up, to find out if there was any news of her and what the police were doing.

When I saw Ann she had still had no news and seemed to have settled into a state of almost resigned depression. If I had not known her as well as I did I might have thought that she had become indifferent to Holly's fate. The truth about it was that the strain of worrying had become too much for her and had brought about a state of hopeless inertia. She had made up her mind to the worst and hardly wanted to be roused to hope.

Hubert was disturbed by her condition and had taken to saying that he was sure that everything would turn out well in the end. Ann seemed not to hear him and when I asked her what the police were doing, only shrugged her shoulders and said, "What can they do?"

Driving Felix home, I gathered that he had had a day of complete idleness. He had attempted to transcribe a tape that Hubert had dictated the day before, but Hubert had told him not to bother with it as he intended to scrap it and cover the ground again in a different way.

"I'd have taken a taxi home if I'd known how to get in touch with you to tell you not to trouble to come and fetch me," he said. "And of course the police were there for a time and I had to wait till they left. Not that I was able to tell them anything."

"Didn't you tell them that you'd seen Holly before?" I asked.

"No," he answered.

"I'm sure you ought to have done that."

He clicked his tongue impatiently. "How often do I have to tell you I don't know anything about her? Just seeing her briefly once—what does that signify?"

"It might help them if you told them about the man you saw her with. You could have done that, couldn't you?"

"Perhaps I could, but I don't see how it would have helped them. He seemed to be a friend of hers, not someone who was likely to do her harm. And that's what they'll be looking for, once they've checked the hospitals hereabouts to find out if any accident cases were brought in yesterday. You may as well face it, Virginia, they'll be thinking of kidnapping and murder. And if it's kidnapping, you know—I mean, if a note demanding a ransom appears in the next few days…"

"Well?" I said as he became silent.

He did not continue at once, but then he said, "I know the police will tell the Brightwells not to pay. They always do. But apart from that, I've a feeling Ann and Hubert ought to be very sure, before they lay out any large sum, that she hasn't arranged the whole thing herself. As a matter of fact, that's what I'm inclined to believe may have happened."

"But in that case the man you saw her with may be an accomplice and you ought to tell the police about him."

He looked as if this had not occurred to him.

"Well, well, you may be right," he said. "I'll think about it."

He had an opportunity to talk to the police again that evening, because soon after we reached home a Detective Inspector Roper called on me to ask if I could tell him anything of interest about Holly. He was a heavily built man with a smooth round face, dark hair receding from a bulging forehead, protuberant eyes, a thick neck, and a cold, incisive voice.

I took him into the sitting room, assuming as I did so that Felix would stay with us, but he disappeared into the kitchen. Apparently he considered that he and Inspector Roper had seen enough of each other that day.

Perhaps the inspector thought so too, for he did not ask for him.

When we had both sat down, he said, "Your friend, Lady Brightwell, will of course have told you of the disappearance of the girl, Holly Noble."

"Yes," I said.

"And you know no more about it than she does?"

"I only know what she's told me."

He nodded. "Yes, of course. But perhaps you can tell me a few things that she couldn't. She's deeply upset and I haven't been able to get any dispassionate picture of the girl from her. And not from Sir Hubert either, because I formed an impression that he had a definite prejudice against Miss Noble. But I thought that a close friend of the family, who's probably seen the girl a number of times, might be able to give me a detached view of her that may be helpful."

I hesitated. "She's very charming."

He looked impatient, as if he had known that I was bound to say that.

"But is she a good-natured girl? Did she confide in you in any way? Had she many friends? Did she talk much about them?"

"I think the answer's 'No' to all those questions," I said, "except that I don't know how good-natured she is. Lady Brightwell's said how kind and considerate she was. But she was very reserved. You might almost say secretive. I never heard her talk about any friends she had, or the life she led before she came here."

"Would you say she was lonely, then?" the inspector asked. "Might she respond if she was accosted by a stranger?"

"I don't know. I don't think so, but I don't know enough about her to tell you anything definite about a thing like that."

"I see." His protuberant eyes were fixed on my face in a stare that I found disconcerting. "She came here out of the blue and she's disappeared into the blue. Would you call that a correct description of what's happened?"

"Except that there's the connection with her mother, which makes her a relation of Lady Brightwell's, so she didn't come exactly out of the blue," I said.

"She came from Rome, where she'd been studying music?"

"So I believe."

"But she's left her violin behind, along with her mink jacket."

"Yes."

"If she'd left voluntarily, I mean with no intention of coming back, would she have left either? Probably both are valuable."

"The mink jacket—no, I don't think she'd have left it. About the violin, I'm not sure she mightn't have left it on purpose. I don't think she'd any genuine interest in music. She said herself that she'd no talent to speak of. She said she wanted to go to a university and study Social Science."

"You never heard her play?"

"No, when Lady Brightwell asked her to she wouldn't. And she seemed to feel that her mother had sent her off to Rome to get her out of the way. I don't know what sort of woman Sara Noble was, but if she was the kind who likes to play down her age, having a daughter of seventeen around the place wouldn't have been very convenient."

"I understand the girl was illegitimate. Do you know anything about the father?"

"Nothing at all."

"Do you know if she ever saw him?"

"I think, occasionally."

"It's just that I've been turning over in my mind whether or not he might have abducted her. Or even if she might have gone to him of her own accord. She never spoke to you about him?"

I shook my head. While we talked I had been trying to make up my mind about how much I ought to tell him of what Felix had told me of having seen the girl sometime before in what even Felix had thought was bad company.

While I was hesitating, the inspector went on, "You know she's been in trouble once about drugs. She and a group of other young people were arrested for being in possession of cannabis. They were all dismissed with a caution, but her case got into the papers because she was Sara Noble's daughter."

"Yes," I said, "I'd heard that."

"You're a physiotherapist," he said.

That took me by surprise. I could see no connection between this fact and what we had been talking about.

"Yes," I said

"Then you've some medical knowledge."

"Very rudimentary," I answered.

"I'm just wondering if, with that rudimentary knowledge, you might have noticed any signs that she was still on drugs," he said.

I shook my head again. "Though when I first heard she'd disappeared I did wonder if she could have gone to London to stock up on them. But it was just a random thought. I'd no evidence for it at all. Actually she looked to me a very healthy girl. But there's something I think perhaps I ought to tell you…"

I paused then because I heard a sound of tapping in the hall. It was the familiar sound of Felix's crutches and the door opened and he came in. I had been about to tell Inspector Roper about the man with whom Felix had seen Holly, but with him there in the room I suddenly felt unable to go on.

He had a grave look on his face and a worried frown, as if while he had been out in the kitchen he had been doing some serious thinking.

"Inspector, I don't know what my wife's been telling you," he said, "but I've come to the conclusion there's something you ought to know about Holly Noble. I might have told you about it when we were over at the Brightwells', but I had my reasons then for keeping it to myself."

Had the unbelievable happened, I wondered. Had Felix for once in his life actually decided to cooperate with the police?

❀ ❀ ❀

It seemed that he had.

Settling himself on the sofa, he went on, "I didn't want to speak about this in front of Sir Hubert and Lady Brightwell because I felt they were likely to think that as soon as I saw the girl I ought to have told them something that I happen to know about her. But she asked me most insistently to say nothing about it. She spoke very movingly of wanting to make a new start and she begged me not to spoil her chances of doing so. And I thought she was sincere, so I agreed. But of course this strange disappearance of hers has altered the situation. Well, the fact is, I saw her once some months ago in a pub in London called the Fox and Grapes, which is in Grieve Street, a turning out of Little Carberry Street, where I live. I didn't even speak to her then, but I recognized the man she was with. He was a character called Norman Redman."

"Redman," the inspector said. "I'll make a note of that." He took a notebook out of his pocket and wrote rapidly. "What do you know about him?"

"Well, I'd had him pointed out to me as a man who was involved with a gang in that neighbourhood who took a rake-off from a lot of local clubs for what I believe is called protection, not to mention a few other forms of wrongdoing. He was an odd-looking man, almost completely bald, with a long white face that looked as if it might be made of putty. Of course I'd no way of knowing how well he and Holly knew one another. He might just have picked her up in the pub a short time before I saw them, or they might have known each other well. She always had a reserved sort of air. It was difficult to guess much about her."

"Thank you, Mr. Freer, that may be very useful," Inspector Roper said.

"And you understand why I didn't tell you about it before?" Felix asked anxiously. Though he had made up his mind during his communion with himself in the kitchen to tell the police what he knew about Holly, it was evident that he did not intend to land himself in any trouble with them that could be avoided.

The inspector nodded, though the way that his bulging eyes dwelt on Felix's face could not have made him feel too easy in his mind.

I drew the detective's attention away from him just then by exclaiming, "The Fox and Grapes! Felix, that's where you said you'd seen those two men whom we saw in the Rose and Crown yesterday evening."

Felix's face immediately became completely blank, except that he gave me one swift, malevolent look. But the inspector was interested.

"More company from the Fox and Grapes?" he said. "Here in Allingford?"

"Yes, they came into the Rose and Crown for a drink," I said. "They didn't stay long. They may only have been passing through. But my husband recognized them and they recognized him and he told me they were burglars."

"Is that so?" the inspector said thoughtfully and looked at Felix as if he were beginning to become curious about the sort of man he was. "What are their names?"

"I don't know," Felix said. "I don't even know for sure they're burglars. It was just the talk in the pub. I think they're brothers and that one of them has just come out of prison after doing a fairly long stretch. But I don't see that they can have anything to do with Holly's disappearance. I've no reason to think she even knew them."

"All the same, I'd like to have their descriptions, if you can give me them." Inspector Roper opened his notebook again and waited expectantly.

Felix gave a helpless shake of his head. "One was big, one was small, I remember that. But that's about all I'm sure of. I'm no good at describing people."

This was certainly untrue, for he is very observant. The inspector turned to me.

"Perhaps you can add something to that, Mrs. Freer."

"I remember that the big one was wearing a pullover with a high roll collar," I said, "and a brown suit that looked too tight for him. Perhaps he'd put on weight while he was in gaol. And I think he was getting on for forty and I remember I noticed that he'd shaved very badly. I don't remember the colour of his hair. I think it was just a sort of mid-brown. But the younger man had fair hair that stood straight up from his forehead and peculiar eyes that had hardly any lashes. I think he was about ten years younger than the big man and he was wearing jeans and a black plastic jacket. That's all I'm sure about."

Inspector Roper gave the first smile that he had given since coming into the room.

"If only more people could be sure of as much as that on other occasions," he said, "it would make life easier for us. Thank you, Mrs. Freer." He stood up, preparing to leave. "It sounds to me as if the chances are that Miss Noble left Allingford voluntarily, going back to the company she's used to. Those two men you've described may have come for her at her own request. It's true it's odd her leaving the mink jacket behind, but that may have been done as a blind, to make us all think just what we've been thinking. It may suit her for a time to stage a complete disappearance. Alternatively, perhaps she'll write to Lady Brightwell soon, asking for her possessions to be sent on to her. I don't believe in the idea of kidnapping myself. She hasn't been with the Brightwells long enough. Her connection with them can't have gone very deep. It's unlikely that they'd pay out a substantial ransom for her. On the other hand, murder, with or without a sexual assault, can't be ruled out at this stage. We've started a very thorough investigation. Thank you both for your help."

He tramped heavily out of the room.

As I returned to the sitting room after letting him out of the front door, Felix exclaimed, "Why the hell did you have to bring those two men into it?"

"Why not?" I asked.

I felt that it was time for a drink and poured one out for myself. If Felix wanted one too, I thought, he could ask for it. But he did not do so.

"Because they won't have had anything to do with kidnapping, or sexual assaults, or murder," he said. "They're professionals. They're burglars. Don't you know there's as much specialization in the criminal classes as there is amongst doctors and lawyers? You wouldn't go to an ophthalmologist to advise you about your arthritis, would you? Well, in the same way you wouldn't go to those two men to carry out a kidnapping for you. If they're here to do a job, it just might have something to do with the Barauds, but it wouldn't have anything to do with Holly."

"If they came for the Barauds," I said, "I don't suppose they knew about the new locks Hubert's had fitted."

"No, and even if they could cope with those, it would still be quite a job, removing *Le Repas en plein air*. It's a bulky thing. They'd have to be able to get it out of the front door and have a van waiting to take it away, which means they'd have to know when the house was empty. And those two Portuguese go out very seldom. If they were around when the men broke in, they'd raise the alarm."

"Unless your friends began by tying them up, or shooting them, or something."

He looked uneasy. "I suppose that's possible. But not likely. Not in their line. No, there's no reason to think they're here to carry off the Barauds. This is a wealthy neighbourhood, isn't it? There must be lots of people around who have things quite as well worth stealing as the Barauds. For instance, take Clyde Crendon. He must be far richer than the Brightwells, and though the way his house is furnished is simple enough, you don't know what he may have in it that might be worth making off with. Suppose he's a collector of rare gems or something he keeps in a safe."

"Of course that could be so," I said. "But in that case, what do you think has happened to Holly?"

Felix looked as if he did not want to have to think about that and suddenly announced that he would like a drink. I poured one out for him and took it to him as he lay on the sofa.

"If it weren't for that mink jacket being left behind, I'd say she's taken off under her own steam," he said. "I've been expecting her to leave sometime soon. But as it is—well, I don't know."

"You don't agree with the inspector that perhaps your two friends came here to pack her up?"

"I wish you wouldn't call them my friends, Virginia. It's rather insulting."

"But you don't think leaving the jacket behind was a blind and that she just wants to disappear for a time."

"A rather expensive blind, wouldn't it be?"

"So you think it's kidnapping or murder."

"Murder, most likely," he answered quietly.

I had been half-expecting it, yet the word stunned me.

After a moment I asked, "Why?"

"Don't you remember what Roper said? He said her connection with the Brightwells can't have gone very deep and that they wouldn't be ready to pay a substantial sum to get her back."

"But he doesn't know Ann."

"You think Ann's already so involved with her that she'd want to pay whatever was asked?"

"I think it's possible."

"But Hubert wouldn't let her."

"I think she's got money of her own. And although she seems such a diffident sort of person, she's very emotional and once she's got her teeth into a thing, she doesn't let go. Hubert usually gives in to her in the end, even if he grumbles about it, just as he did about inviting Holly to come."

"But the kidnappers wouldn't know that. If they're professionals at the job, they probably wouldn't think of her as a very promising prospect."

"Someone who would know it is Holly herself."

Felix's eyebrows went up. He sipped some whiskey, then gave a sardonic laugh.

"So you've come round to thinking there's something in my idea that Holly planted herself here with the intention of worming her way into Ann's affections, having arranged beforehand to have herself kidnapped to raise a nice lump of cash. I'd have thought she'd have inherited enough from her mother to satisfy her, but perhaps there wasn't much. All the same, even though that was my own idea, I've got doubts about it."

"Why?" I asked.

"You're always saying why, like a three-year-old child," he said. "Well, simply because, as Roper pointed out, she disappeared too soon. If she really made a cold-blooded plan to exploit Ann's feelings, she'd have played it safe and stayed on till she was much more confident of Ann's affection than she can be yet. She'd have stayed at least another month or two."

"But perhaps there were reasons why she couldn't wait. Perhaps she needed the money quickly. For instance, suppose she's got a boyfriend who's got to get out of the country in a hurry, someone who's wanted by the police, perhaps, and who wants to get away to one of those safe countries that haven't any extradition treaty with us. Then she might gamble on getting the money soon so that she could go with him."

He gave another laugh. "You've really quite an imagination when you let yourself go. More than I've ever given you credit for. But I think I'll be conservative and stick to the theory that it's murder."

"Without any motive? Just the pickup, the sexual assault, then probably strangling and her body dumped where it may not be found for a year or two, if ever."

"Isn't that the usual explanation when young girls disappear, unless they've gone off of their own free will?"

I felt a shiver run up my spine, but I was just about to agree with him when the doorbell rang.

Picking up one of his crutches, Felix thumped with it on the floor in an unusual display of anger. He very seldom loses his temper.

"If that's the police back again, for God's sake deal with them on the doorstep and don't let them in," he said. "I've had enough of them today."

But it was not the police, it was Clyde Crendon, wearing an old mackintosh over a pullover and shabby trousers and with his round, pink face looking unusually pale and almost hollow-cheeked in the light that fell on it from the hall. His sparse, straw-coloured hair looked damp and I saw that it was again raining heavily. The circle of light from the open door lit up the slanting shafts of the rain as they came driving down through the darkness. I began to feel as if it had been raining for days and perhaps would never stop, as there might never be any solution to Holly's disappearance. Somewhere the rain might be drenching her dead body, undiscovered.

"Am I a nuisance?" Clyde asked. "Are you awfully busy? I came because I felt I'd got to talk to someone. You know what's happened, of course."

"You mean about Holly's disappearing?" I said.

He nodded and seemed to have nothing to add to it. At lease he had not come to tell us that Holly's corpse had been found.

"I've just been to the Brightwells," he said. "I went to return a book. And they told me how she'd vanished, and there was a policeman there and he asked me the most extraordinary questions about how well I knew her, and had I known her mother, and even if I knew who her father was. And I felt so upset after it that I thought I couldn't just go home, so I thought of coming here, but if I'm a nuisance—"

"Of course not," I interrupted. "Come in."

He stepped into the hall and took off his mackintosh. Though his car was at the gate and he had had to walk up only the short path to the door, there was a shiny look of dampness on his face as well as his hair. Taking a handkerchief out of a pocket, he mopped his high, smooth forehead. I took him into the sitting room where he greeted Felix with an absent frown, as if it was vaguely puzzling to find him there.

"I feel so terribly sorry for Lady Brightwell," he said. "She seems to have become quite confused and distraught. Shock, I suppose. Of course she hadn't known the girl long, but she'd really set her heart on making a success of the relationship, hadn't she? And she seemed almost anxious that the girl's disappearance should turn out to be kidnapping, as if that would at least be better than some other possibilities."

I asked him what he would like to drink and he asked for whiskey.

As I was pouring it out, he went on, "What do you yourselves think happened?"

"We don't know any more about it than you do," I said.

"It seems to me that to be kidnapped in a place like Allingford, if you aren't a child who hasn't learnt yet not to speak to strangers, you'd have to be a certain sort of person." He took the glass from me and sat down. "Someone, I mean, who'd accept a lift from a stranger. In other words, rather naïve, or—well, used to doing that sort of thing, if you see what I mean."

"In fact, used to responding, as a matter of course, to kerb-crawlers," I said.

"Well, yes." He looked embarrassed at what he himself had suggested. "What was your impression of the girl?"

I waited for Felix to answer, as he certainly knew more about Holly than I did, but he did not seem inclined to speak. So I said, "That's what Inspector Roper was asking us a little time ago. We hadn't much to tell him."

"Then she didn't talk much to you about herself?" Clyde asked.

"Hardly at all. And that's about all we were able to tell the inspector—that we never heard her talk about her background, her time in Rome, her friends, or anything like that."

"Would you say she was actually secretive?"

"I think that's the word I used."

"And of course you think I'm being peculiarly inquisitive," he said, "but it's a habit I've got, I suppose connected with being a writer. I always want to find out all I can about people. And for some reason she intrigued me from the start. She seemed to me—well, I don't know if it'll make sense to you, but she seemed to me to be the sort of person to whom things happen."

Felix suddenly decided to enter the conversation. "She may have been picked up by someone she knew."

Clyde gave a little start, as if he had forgotten that Felix was in the room.

"Yes—yes, of course that's possible," he said, but he sounded taken aback. "And if that's what happened there wouldn't have been any shocking scene in the middle of Allingford. It's been puzzling me, how that could have been managed. But do you mean it's a fake kidnapping?"

"Calling it a kidnapping when we've still no evidence about it is going a bit too fast, isn't it?" Felix said.

"I think it was a kidnapping," Clyde said. "I'm sure it was." He finished his whiskey quickly and stood up. "Poor girl, whatever it was. Now I won't bother you any longer. I'm afraid I've been a nuisance. But I do believe it was kidnapping. I feel it in my bones. Perhaps that's only because the alternatives are so much worse. But no, I'm sure I'm right."

I saw him to the door and out once more into the pouring rain.

When he had gone I went to the kitchen to carve the remains of the chicken that we had had the evening before and to make a salad to go with it, and while I was doing it I heard the tapping of Felix's crutches crossing the hall and a moment later I saw him at the door.

"Why d'you think he really came?" he asked.

I was washing a lettuce under the tap.

"Perhaps he feels exciting things have been happening and he's been left out of them," I suggested.

"I suppose that could be it," Felix said dubiously.

"He is very inquisitive, you know. Look at the questions he asked me about you the other day."

"But I don't believe he came to us just because of his general interest in the human race, for literary purposes," he said. "I've a queer feeling he actually wanted to find out if we knew anything about Holly."

"Whyever should he want that?"

"I don't know. I rather wish I did."

"It's just what you feel in your bones, is it? Like him, you've got informative bones."

"Perhaps I have."

"Anyway, I bought another of his books today," I said. "I can't really explain it, because they aren't really my sort of thing at all, but once I start one I can't stop. They could easily become an addiction. But if Holly's disappearance was happening in one of them I know her corpse would turn up chopped into half a dozen pieces in various London sewers. And some clever forensic scientist would be able to prove that she'd been raped and tortured and mutilated before she was killed. Yet he seems such a gentle little man."

"Just a very successful case of sublimation," Felix said. "Dig deep enough down and you'd probably find he's a seething mass of aggression."

"Aren't we all?"

"Oh, not me," Felix said. "There's next to no aggression in me. You'd have been far happier with me if there'd been more. You're a very aggressive woman and you respect aggression in others."

For once I was inclined to think that there might be a certain amount of truth in this, so I did not argue.

I took my new Clyde Crendon book up to bed with me and, as I had done with the one before it, went on reading until nearly one o'clock, and as a result slept late. I was wakened by the ringing of the telephone.

"Virginia, it's come!" Ann's voice said excitedly. "The kidnap letter. It was in the post this morning. They say she's safe and that they won't harm her for the present, but to get her back safe and sound we've got to pay two hundred thousand pounds before next Sunday!"

# Chapter Five

When I went downstairs I found Felix still asleep on the divan in the sitting room. I woke him.

"Ann's just telephoned," I said. "She said a letter's come in this morning's post saying that if they want to get Holly back safe and sound they've got to pay two hundred thousand pounds."

Felix grunted, trying to fight off my interruption of his comfortable slumber. I repeated what I had said.

He opened his eyes. "Seems a modest sum, considering inflation," he said.

"I'm going to get breakfast," I said, "and you'd better get up. I think we should go over there as soon as we can."

"And I'd decided to stay here today," he said. "Hubert isn't in a mood for work at the moment."

"If you don't want to come, I'll go by myself," I said. "Ann needs a bit of support."

"Oh, I'll come, though I don't see what good we can do." He sat up and reached for his dressing gown. "The police will take over firmly from now on."

I went out to the kitchen and made toast and coffee. When it was ready I put it on a tray and took it to the sitting room. By then Felix had got as far as putting on his dressing gown, but he was still sitting on the edge of his bed.

"You know, that autobiography's never going to get written," he said. "I may as well go home."

"But how about your leg?" I asked. "Could you cope?"

"I suppose I could if I had to. You'd like me to go, wouldn't you? There's a certain waspish note that gets into your voice when you've had enough of me."

"I don't want you to go till I'm sure you can manage."

"That's magnanimous of you. But I believe I could manage now. I'm feeling a lot better than when I arrived. For one thing I've got used to the feeling of having a ton of plaster on my leg. And there's a nice girl called Hermione who's moved into the top floor flat at Little Carberry Street who's said she'll always do any shopping I want, so things shouldn't be too difficult."

I poured out coffee for us both and gave him toast and marmalade.

"Why d'you really want to go?" I asked. "Are you pining for the nice girl in the top flat, or has it something to do with the letter the Brightwells had this morning?"

"There you are," he said, "the waspish note."

"Has it anything to do with the letter? You said the police will be taking over and you've never cared much for being on familiar terms with them."

"It's got nothing to do with the letter and it's got nothing to do with Hermione. It's just that both Hubert and I are fed up with trying to write that book. He never realized what hard work it was going to be. He thought all that could be left to me, but of course I'm not much help. And now he's going to use all this kidnapping excitement as an alibi for not going on. So I think I may as well leave before I'm sacked."

"There's something in that," I said. "Perhaps you should go."

"But I'll go over there with you this morning if you want me to and don't mind waiting while I get dressed. Two hundred thousand. Well, well." He stood up. "You know, it's a sombre thought that there's no one on earth who would pay two hundred thousand to get me back. I suppose that means I've made a failure of my life. And yet I keep hoping that sooner or later I'll find the right track to follow and be loved and successful."

"There aren't many people who've that amount to spare," I said. "I wonder if the Brightwells have."

"Even if they have, the police won't let them pay it," Felix said and, picking up his crutches, hobbled out of the room to shave and get dressed.

It was about half past nine when we arrived at the Brightwells' house. Santos let us in, took us to the drawing room and announced us in funereal tones, as if he were aware of tragedy hanging over the house. For once Ann had not come hurrying out to meet me but had remained standing by the fire, and she looked at me now with a puzzled stare. She might have been wondering what I was doing there and I began to have doubts that perhaps I should not have come. Her short grey hair was dishevelled as if she had forgotten to comb it that morning.

"Oh, Virginia, I thought you were the police," she said. "Hubert rang them and told them about the letter and Inspector Roper's coming, and I suppose he'll tell us what we ought to do. But I can't think—I simply can't *think*—what one can possibly do but pay."

Hubert was standing in the bay window, his hands in his pockets, his forehead creased in a frown.

"I don't know where you think the money's coming from," he said.

"We've got it—we've got more than that," Ann said.

"Money we've put by to help in our old age," he said. "We're to part with it, are we, to get back a girl we've only known for a couple of weeks?"

"But, Hubert, if we don't, they may *kill* her," Ann said, her voice unusually high-pitched and shaking. She held out a piece of paper to me. "Here's the letter, Virginia. What do you think of it?"

It was, I supposed, the sort of letter to be expected in the circumstances. The words had all been cut out from newspapers and pasted onto a sheet of cheap, lined paper which for certain would be untraceable.

It said, *"Holly safe will be returned to you unharmed if you pay two hundred thousand pounds by Sunday instructions as to payment will follow do not communicate police."*

"But you have communicated with the police," I said as I handed it on to Felix.

"Oh yes," Ann answered. "Hubert insisted on our doing that at once."

"There was an announcement about her disappearance on the seven o'clock news this morning," he said. "No actual mention of kidnapping, because we hadn't had the letter yet, but they described her and what she was wearing and asked anyone in Allingford who thought they'd seen her to get in touch with them, so the kidnappers will know they're on the case already. But we'd have had to call them in anyhow. One can't handle this sort of thing oneself. And I suspect they'll tell us not to pay at any price. But if they don't, if they say go ahead and pay if that's what you want to do, there's only one way to raise the money and that's by selling the Barauds. And if that's what Ann wants to do, I shan't protest, but I'm damned if I'll pay out a lot of our hard-earned savings to a gang of crooks."

"You would if she were your daughter," Ann said.

"She is *not* my daughter!"

They looked at each other with a kind of hatred. I had seen them look at each other in that way before over minor disagreements and thought that the antagonism between them did not go deep. It is so much the most comfortable thing to assume that the marriages of one's friends are fairly successful. But now I felt shaken.

The doorbell rang and Hubert said, "That'll be the police."

It was Inspector Roper and he was accompanied by a young man whom he introduced as Sergeant Michaels, a big, well-built, bullet-headed man of about thirty who knew, it was evident, that his job at the moment was to stay in the background. Felix had handed the letter from the kidnappers back to Ann and she handed it now to the inspector.

He asked her if she still had the envelope and she picked one up that had been lying on the mantelpiece and gave it to him.

He glanced at it and said, "Posted in London. As you might expect. An anonymous place, London. I'll keep these." He put them into a wallet and added, "You aren't thinking of paying up."

"That's what we thought you'd say," Hubert said. "You think we shouldn't?"

"Not on any account," the inspector answered. "But at present all you can do is wait for the instructions you've been promised. When they come, which will be on the telephone, don't say you won't pay. Protest, if you like, argue, but don't say definitely you won't pay and get him to talk for as long as you can. Probably you won't be successful. He'll say about two sentences and ring off. Then get in touch with us immediately and tell us exactly what he said and after that we'll have to play it by ear. It may be it'll be best to seem to go along with him."

"Inspector, do you think..." Ann began diffidently, then caught her breath and stopped.

"Yes?" he said in a kindlier tone than I had thought him capable of.

"Do you think that even if we paid we'd get her back?" she asked.

He made a gesture with one hand that expressed only helplessness.

"It's impossible to say. One hopes for the best. But if she can identify the kidnappers, she's probably in grave danger. And not to delude you, I think I ought to add that there's always the possibility that she's dead already. Until we've some idea of the kind of people we're dealing with, we can't begin to guess. I wish I could give you more encouragement. But kidnapping, in my view, is about the nastiest, as well as the most difficult sort of crime we ever have to deal with. I'm thankful to say I haven't much experience of it. But we'll do all we can to help. Trust us, Lady Brightwell, and please don't take any action without consulting us."

"No," she said, but with a sound of deep reluctance. "No, of course not."

The inspector and the sergeant departed.

Dropping into a chair, crouching in it and taking her head in her hands, Ann murmured something inaudibly. Hubert asked her what she had said. She did not answer at first, but then she sat back in the chair and gave a deep sigh.

"I was only saying that now we've got to wait for the telephone to ring. And you know how it'll be. Everyone we know will choose just today to ring us up. And every time we hear it we'll think it's the terrible man we're expecting, but it'll just be someone who wants to chat. And we'll have to ask them please to get off the line because we're expecting an important call. And then perhaps he won't ring at all, though we'll go on staying up right through the night in case he does."

At that moment the telephone rang.

Jerking violently in her chair, Ann started to scramble to her feet, but before she could do so Hubert had reached the telephone and picked it up.

"Oh," he said after a moment. "Yes...Yes, of course...' Glad to see you." He put down the telephone. "Barbie," he said. "She and Tim are coming over."

"You see what I mean," Ann said. "That's how it'll go on. Of course I don't mind Tim and Barbie coming, but if anyone else rings up, Hubert, for heaven's sake tell them we can't see them. I couldn't bear it. We don't know how many people listened to the seven o'clock news and who's going to want to come and sympathize, or just ask maddening questions, and I couldn't—I really couldn't bear it."

"If I might say something," Felix said hesitantly.

She turned her head to give him a blank stare, as if she could not imagine what he was doing in the room.

"I don't say it's probable," he said, "but Virginia and I have been talking it over and we don't think we ought to overlook the possibility that Holly arranged this kidnapping herself. Until the note came I didn't believe it. To be honest with you, I thought it was going to turn out to be murder. I thought she must have been picked up and no doubt raped and strangled and dumped somewhere. One's always hearing about that kind of thing nowadays. But the note shows I was wrong. All the same, somehow I can't believe in it."

Hubert, looking very stern, nodded. "My own feeling exactly."

"You see, kidnapping is a rather complex sort of crime," Felix went on. "You have to know a good many things in advance to make it worth your while. First, have your victims got the sort of money you're going to demand? Can they actually pay? How can you be sure of that? Second, do they care enough for the character you've spirited away to pay out what you ask? You can't really be sure of that either, can you? Third, can you arrange the pickup of the money in such a way that the police won't grab you the moment you lay your hands on it? And anyway, won't the money probably be in forged notes, or at least in marked ones, so that spending any of it will only lead to serious trouble? No, I don't think kidnapping would be my favourite crime, unless the stakes were enormous."

Felix had been smoking and now stubbed his cigarette out in an ashtray near him, looking down at it thoughtfully before lighting another.

"I suppose if I thought I might get away with a million or two," he said, "I might be tempted to try my hand at it. But two hundred thousand, as things go nowadays, isn't such a vast sum. But I can just imagine that Holly herself might have settled on the sum because she thought it was just about as high as you'd go. She lived with you long enough to know that you could raise the money without impoverishing yourselves seriously simply by selling the Barauds. An amateur sort of crime, of course, though quite promising for a beginner. Leaving her mink jacket behind was a neat touch."

Ann went on looking at him for a moment without speaking, then at last she said, "Are you serious?"

I was wondering about that myself. I had recognized by now the role that Felix was playing, though he had so many roles which he preferred playing to being simply himself, and he could switch from one to the other so quickly without even being aware himself of what he was doing, that it could be hard to be sure of what he was up to. But at the moment, I knew, he was being the great detective. But that did not necessarily mean that it would be wise to dismiss what he had said. He could be disconcertingly perceptive, even when he was play-acting. All the same, Ann's question seemed to embarrass him.

"I think so," he said. "Yes, I think so."

Hubert strode across the room to the bell.

"I think we'll have some coffee," he said. "I need it. With all this damned agitation this morning, I feel as if I'd been up since dawn."

Ann was still looking at Felix thoughtfully. "So you think the right thing for us to do at the moment is nothing at all. Not to sell the Barauds?"

"Well, what you do is up to you," he said.

"Yes," she said, "and I think I know what I'll do. But there's no point in going on discussing it for the moment."

We were drinking coffee when Tim and Barbie arrived. Barbie ran in ahead of Tim, threw her arms round Ann and kissed her lovingly.

"Oh, Ann darling, we're so sorry for you," she said. "We heard about it on the seven o'clock news this morning. But why didn't you let us know yourselves what had happened?"

Ann was unresponsive to her embrace. In a flat voice she said, "There was a letter this morning demanding money for Holly's safe return, but the police think she may be dead already."

"So you've brought the police in on it," Tim said. "I suppose that was wise."

"Of course," she answered. "What else could we do?"

"May I see the letter?" he asked.

"The police have taken it. But all it said was that if we wanted her back safe and sound we'd have to pay two hundred thousand pounds and that we were to wait for further instructions."

"It's horrible!" Barbie exclaimed. "You aren't going to pay it!"

"There's only one way we could," Hubert said, "and that's by selling the Barauds. Not that I have anything against that in a general way, but I'd like to be sure I was going to get value for my money. I shouldn't like to pay it and then have a corpse delivered at my door."

Ann clapped her hands over her ears. "Don't, don't, don't!" she shrieked. "You make the poor girl sound like—like a commodity. Value for money—oh, my God! Isn't life, *any* human life, worth all the money one's got?"

Tim had sat down on the sofa, had accepted a cup of coffee, and was looking at Ann with a troubled frown on his long, thin face.

"So you're thinking of paying, Ann," he said sombrely. "That's what you really want to do."

"Perhaps it is," she said in a calmer voice. "If only I could be sure…"

"Sure that you'll get her back alive?"

She nodded. "And that she hasn't helped with the kidnapping herself."

"That's an extraordinary idea," he said.

"It's what Felix thinks she's done," she said. "He thinks she arranged it and that it's just a way of getting money out of us. And I don't see how we can tell what it is. Oh, I think kidnapping is the most wicked crime there is. It's much worse than blackmail. It's worse than murder."

"It's for the police to find out what's really happened," Hubert said. "We can't decide anything till we've had the instructions the kidnappers said they'd give us and talked them over with the police."

"Well, if you want to sell the Barauds, I can tell you who'd buy them," Tim said with a sardonic little laugh. "Our new friend, Clyde Crendon. He's crazy about the things. And I think he could write a cheque for you on the spot."

Barbie had sat down beside him and gave him a nudge with her elbow.

He seemed to know what the nudge meant, for he went on, "I'm sorry, Ann, I shouldn't have said that. I know you haven't got as far as thinking about that sort of thing yet. And I don't really know if Crendon would be interested, even if the pictures were offered to him. I'm a fool. I'm sorry."

Barbie nodded. "Yes, darling, sometimes you can be a terrible fool. You've just been excelling yourself."

But she said it affectionately and as I saw them sitting side by side I thought how wonderfully satisfying it must be to have a marriage like theirs. I always had the feeling when I was with them that they had an understanding of one another that was almost as if they could communicate in some private code. Looking at Felix and thinking how handsome he was, and how charming he could be, and how much I had once been in love with him, I recognized sadly that even at that time we had never experienced anything like the intuitive union that there was between Tim and Barbie.

And neither had Ann and Hubert. In this crisis they were hardly any help to one another. In fact, it seemed to me, it was bringing to the surface that latent hostility which I had sensed in their relationship.

"Mind you, if the Barauds were mine, I'd sell them," Tim went on, but his tone had altered. It sounded as if he were merely making conversation and not talking about the kidnapping anymore. "It would scare me to death, having anything so valuable in the house. As things are, Barbie and I can leave the cottage or our flat standing empty for weeks without worrying about a possible break-in. I expect it would be horrid enough if there were one, especially if it were done by the kind of lunatic who leaves excrement on the carpet and fouls the walls, but we're comfortably free of anything irreplaceable."

"Fortunately for us," Hubert said, "the house is very seldom completely empty. Santos and his wife have their odd day off, but the chances are that Ann or I will be at home at the time—"

He broke off as the doorbell sounded.

We were all expecting the police again, and when Santos ushered in a tall, thin, bald man, muttered something in his inadequate English which was presumably the newcomer's name and left him to us, I think we all assumed that the stranger was a detective. A more senior detective, probably, than Inspector Roper, for he had an air of authority that the inspector had not yet acquired.

He stood still just inside the door, looking round at us curiously. He was about fifty and was still good-looking, with a well-shaped head so that his baldness was not disfiguring, an oval face with strong, regular features and deep-set, intelligent brown eyes. His eyebrows were thick and dark and it seemed that the little that was left of his hair, which was now grey, had also once been dark. He was wearing a dark suit which was well cut but somewhat dated, which somehow helped to give him a look of distinction.

"I must apologize for intruding on you," he said. "I must introduce myself. I am Lionel Ilsley."

He had a soft, cultured voice, and though I expect a good many detectives have soft, cultured voices, his sounded wrong for a member of the police force. There was also the curious fact that it sounded as if he thought that we would know the name.

"Yes?" Hubert said and waited for further enlightenment.

The stranger saw that we were puzzled.

"Holly never spoke of me?" he said.

"I don't believe so," Hubert answered.

"I see. I thought she might have done so. But if she never did, perhaps I ought not to have come. I heard the news of her disappearance on the radio this morning and got in touch with the police immediately and they directed me to you. Not that I suppose I can be of any help to you, but naturally I'm deeply concerned at what's happened and hope that you can tell me more about it. You see, I'm Holly's father."

There was a moment of silence, then Ann held out a hand to him.

"I'm Ann Brightwell," she said. "A remote cousin of Holly's. It was I who invited her to come here. It's true she didn't speak of you by name, though we understood she saw you occasionally. She never told us anything much about her background. If we'd known who you were of course we'd have got in touch with you as soon as this horrible thing happened."

"In any case, you'd probably have thought I didn't want to be involved." He gave a sad smile. "The truth is, it's been one of the sorrows of my life that I couldn't see far more of the child than I did. I loved her and I loved her mother. But I've a wife and other children too and one of the terms my wife made for continuing our marriage, which I wanted for the sake of those others, was that they shouldn't know of Holly's existence. It made it very difficult for me to see her. Now, perhaps, I should leave. You may not find this story edifying."

"Oh, you mustn't go," Ann said quickly. I could see that she had warmed to him at once, though Hubert was looking him up and down as if he certainly did not find the story edifying. "Come and sit down. We were just drinking coffee. You'll have some, won't you? I understand how you must feel and I wish we had something helpful for you, but we're still quite in the dark ourselves." She rang the bell for Santos and asked him to bring another cup. "Did the police tell you about the letter we had this morning?"

Lionel Ilsley sat down in the chair that was nearest to the one to which she had returned, as if he felt that she was his best friend in the room.

"No," he said.

"They've taken it away, so we can't show it to you," Ann went on. "But it was a letter from the kidnappers, saying she'd be returned to us unharmed if we paid two hundred thousand pounds. They said instructions about how we were to do this would follow."

"I see. And of course you don't know what to do. The police have probably told you not to pay."

"They've told us to wait and see what the instructions are."

As if he recognized Hubert's hostility to him, the newcomer turned his head to address him directly.

"Perhaps I ought to tell you a little more about myself. If you should decide to pay, and of course I'll accept your decision on that matter, I can help towards producing that sum they've asked for, but I can't possibly lay my hands on the whole of it. I would if I could."

"It isn't inability to raise the money that's worrying us," Hubert said stiffly, as if he resented the suggestion that he might not have such a sum available, "but a doubt as to the wisdom of paying it at all."

"Ah yes, that's always the trouble in the cases one hears of, though of course one doesn't know what's gone on behind the scenes. It would naturally be inadvisable to advertise the fact that any money's been paid over. It would only encourage other kidnappers. But perhaps more money changes hands than one ever hears about."

Lionel Ilsley smoothed a hand over his high, bald forehead. He looked as if he were trying to erase the wrinkles that streaked it horizontally above his heavy eyebrows.

"I was going to tell you a little more about myself, however. To have someone of whom you know nothing intruding on you at a time like this may be distressing. I'm a schoolmaster. To be precise, headmaster of a school called Endersfield. You may have heard of it. It's a progressive school in Dorset which my wife and I founded between us and it's largely due to her, I'm sure, that it's been a very satisfactory success. It was with her money that we were able to start it and, ironically enough, it was at her suggestion that we presumed to invite Sara Noble and a small group of other actors to visit us and give a brief performance to the children. I was amazed when she accepted, though of course she was not yet as famous as she later became. I remember they performed some excerpts from *Comus* in our very lovely gardens, and I was moved beyond words. And that's how I first met Sara. And she seemed to fall in love with me.

Actually it was hardly serious and it was over so soon that I look back on it now as something that could never really have happened. But there was Holly..."

He broke off as Ann handed him a cup of coffee.

"I beg your pardon," he said. "I don't know why I'm talking like this. All I meant to tell you was that I'm a schoolmaster, that I once had a brief affair with Sara Noble, that Holly is my child, and that I will do anything I can to help in the present circumstances."

"I suppose Holly didn't go to your school," Ann said.

"Oh no," he answered. "Naturally I wanted it, but my wife wouldn't hear of it. Holly went to a school in Suffolk which she left young because she was a child who matured early and it was a waste of time and money keeping her there. And from early childhood she's been dedicated to the violin. The only thing she ever wanted was a chance to study it seriously. So Sara sent her to an academy in Rome. But before she went there..."

He hesitated and looked round at us all, as if it had just occurred to him to check on the effect his story was having.

"Well, you may have read an account of it in the papers," he said. "If she hadn't been Sara's daughter no notice would have been taken of it. But though Sara did her best to shield her from the publicity, it got out. The child had been arrested with a group of others for smoking pot. And that was partly why Sara sent her to Rome instead of to the Royal College of Music here. But it can't have been too successful, or she wouldn't have wanted to give it up to come home. There was no problem about the fees. Sara had always paid them, but when she died I wrote at once to Holly and told her that of course I'd continue to do it and that she need not be concerned about her future. But she told me then she'd been in touch with you and that you'd very kindly invited her to stay with you. To tell you the truth, I pleaded with her not to do anything in a hurry. She's so talented, you see. I hated the thought that might go to waste. But she was quite positive that she wanted to come back to England. I'm afraid she's basically a rather unstable girl and that she may have a difficult time ahead of her."

"If she's got any life at all," Felix observed.

It startled me. It was not like him. He was not usually callous. Some of the more fantastic tales he told about himself came down to the fact, when you examined them, that he was trying to spare someone's feelings. But he was looking at Lionel Ilsley with an expression of grim dislike. I knew that this could have nothing to do with the moral backsliding that had resulted in Holly, because Felix was always ready to let other people arrange their emotional affairs as they liked, but I could see that there was something about the other man that had aroused strong animosity in him.

"As you say," Lionel Ilsley replied gravely. "If she's going to come out of this horrible situation safely." He turned to Ann again. "May I ask you, what did you make of her? I've always worried a great deal that her unfortunate background would do her some serious damage. Not that Sara didn't do her best for her, but what's called a one-parent family nowadays, particularly when the one parent happens to be a very famous actress, can't supply much of what a child really needs. But on the rare occasions when we were able to meet, it always seemed to me that Holly had survived surprisingly well. Perhaps environment isn't as important as we educationists tend to think. In the end it may come down to just a question of the stuff we're made of."

"I liked her very much," Ann said. "I took to her at once."

"I'm very glad to hear you say so."

"Of course, she was very shy, very reserved. It wasn't easy to start a relationship with her."

"That surprises me," he said. "I thought her almost the reverse, so gay and warm and forthcoming. She loved to chatter to me about her school and her friends and what she was doing, and she was always so interested in other people."

"Well, after all, we were strangers," Ann said. "I expect she'd soon have overcome her nervousness of us."

"Or perhaps she's just a classic case of the manic depressive," Tim suggested. "Could that explain what's happened to her?"

"I don't understand," Lionel Ilsley said.

"Well, if the depressive phase came on while she was here, mightn't she simply have wandered away in a state of desperation and despair, and really not known what she was doing?"

"You're forgetting the kidnap letter," Barbie said. "Somebody's got hold of her."

"Yes, of course. Stupid of me," Tim agreed.

"Though perhaps if she was in that state," Barbie went on, "she'd be glad to talk to a sympathetic stranger and would let him do what he liked with her."

"If she wanted sympathy," Hubert said harshly, "she'd plenty of it here. I'm inclined to agree with Felix that Holly may have cooperated in this kidnapping and she's just waiting somewhere happily for us to be fools enough to pay up."

"*Holly* cooperated in this kidnapping?" Lionel Ilsley said incredulously. "You can't be serious. She isn't like that at all. She's transparently honest. And there's no trace of the manic depressive about her either. She's a normal, cheerful, friendly girl whom everyone likes. If what you're thinking about is that drug business—"

He broke off as the front door bell rang again.

I heard the opening and shutting of the door, then footsteps crossing the hall, then Inspector Roper and Sergeant Michaels were ushered into the drawing room.

I noticed a change about them at once. It was a change that instantly made me apprehensive, though I could not have said what it was. There was a hard look of concentration about the inspector as he looked round at us all which suggested that anything that we said or did would be noted and might be used in evidence. The young sergeant looked both excited and scared, as if something that was happening was outside his experience, but he knew that he ought not to show this.

Inspector Roper stood still just inside the door.

"I'm afraid I've some very bad news for you," he said. "It reached us only a short time ago and I came here as quickly as I could to tell you what it is. I'll tell it to you simply. News like this can't be broken gently. We've heard from the Sussex police that the body of Holly Noble has been found in a pond near the town of East Wellfleet. Some boys who'd gone fishing there found her. But she had not been drowned. Before she was dropped into the water her throat had been cut."

A moan that was a sound of protest broke from Ann. Then she clapped a hand over her mouth to hold in what might have followed.

The inspector gave her a thoughtful look in which there was a grave sympathy, and went on, "Most of her clothing had been stripped away, but there's no evidence of a sexual assault. It looks as if the clothing was removed with the object of preventing identification. However, the Metropolitan police had her fingerprints in their files, and without question the body is that of Holly Noble. I'm truly sorry to bring you this news, Lady Brightwell, and sorry too, Sir Hubert, that there's something I must ask you to do. We have no doubt as to the identity of the dead girl, all the same it's necessary that we should have a formal identification of her by someone who knew her. If you'll come with us, if possible at once, we can drive you over to East Wellfleet and bring you back again in only two or three hours."

Lionel Ilsley had sprung to his feet. He looked as if he wanted to interrupt the inspector violently but could not get the words out. At last they came.

"Holly—Holly's body—Holly's fingerprints! How the hell did you get her fingerprints? How the hell do you know this poor girl is really Holly?"

Inspector Roper turned his hard stare onto him, then looked questioningly at Hubert, wanting to know who the stranger was.

Lionel Ilsley saved him the trouble of answering.

"I'm Holly's father, damn it!" he shouted. "My name's Ilsley—Lionel Ilsley—and if anyone's going to identify her, it'll be me. But I don't believe for a moment it's Holly you've found. Those fingerprints you're talking about, how could they be hers?"

"The Metropolitan police have had them ever since she was arrested on a drugs charge," Inspector Roper answered. "And I'm afraid the evidence is positive, though it's true there are certain circumstances in the case which are difficult to explain…" He paused. "Naturally if you'll come with us too, sir, we'll be grateful, but I should like Sir Hubert to come, just to help us to clear up one or two things we don't understand. You're coming, Sir Hubert?"

"Yes, yes, immediately," Hubert said.

Then he did something that took me by surprise. He walked across the room and kissed Ann on the cheek. He also patted her shoulder. He did it awkwardly, as if gestures of tenderness did not come easily to him. Then he and Lionel Ilsley and the two detectives left the room.

# Chapter Six

We were all still for a moment, then Ann gave a strange little cry and ran out of the room.

I heard her running up the stairs and waited to see if Barbie, who after all was a closer connection of Ann's than I was, was going to follow her, but Barbie only moved closer to Tim, her face very white and her mouth forming a syllable which did not come out as a sound, but which looked as if she were crying "No!"

So I went after Ann up the stairs and to her bedroom. I remembered which room it was from the days when I had been giving her massage and instructing her in the exercises that she should do after her operation. She and Hubert slept in separate rooms. The door of his faced hers across the passage and stood open, but she had closed hers behind her.

I tapped on it, then as I did not hear any reply, I opened it and went into the room.

She was standing at the window, a curved bay which overlooked the garden at the back of the house. It had a dismal look today, for although it was not raining, the sky was overcast with sullen clouds moving slowly across it and a slight wind bending the branches of the trees which were still bare, although the forsythia and the daffodils promised that spring was coming.

Ann turned when she heard me come in and I saw that she was crying.

"You were very fond of her then," I said, "even though you'd known her such a short time."

She started to mop her face with a handkerchief.

"I didn't even like her," she answered. Her voice was thickened by her tears. "But what difference does that make now?"

"I thought you liked her very much," I said. "I remember your saying how kind and considerate she was."

"Oh, what I *said*!" She spoke scornfully. "I was trying. I tried awfully hard. I was determined to make it work. But she was impossible. Ice-cold. You couldn't make friends with her."

"Then why the tears? Just shock? That's understandable. It's an appallingly shocking thing to have happened."

She turned towards the window again and spoke with her back to me.

"Yes, perhaps it's shock. Partly, anyway. But mostly it's because..." She broke off and pressed both her fists to her mouth, keeping the next words from coming out. Then after a moment she let her hands fall and gave a long sigh. "It's because I'm such a failure at everything. And I wanted so terribly to make this thing with Holly a success. I know that was a leftover of my not being able to have children, and Hubert told me that it wouldn't work and would only lead to trouble, and of course he was right, but I wanted to show him that he wasn't always right about everything, and now—and now—" She choked.

"It wasn't your fault that the poor girl was kidnapped and murdered," I said.

"I feel as if it was. If she'd been happier with us she wouldn't have picked up with some strange man and gone off with him—because that must be how it happened, mustn't it? She was bored and lonely and she didn't like me, so she just went off with some stranger."

"I should think it's the kind of background she had that's to blame, not you," I said.

"That's what Hubert's been saying ever since she disappeared. And it's made me so furious, because I was trying so hard to get the girl to understand that what I was offering her was affection, real affection, without any strings to it, and that she should try to trust me, even if she'd never done such a thing before. I don't think she ever had, you know. I believe it was like what happens to children who grow up in institutions, even the best of them. They've never experienced the sort of intimacy that comes from affection, so they don't even want it. She seemed almost scared when I tried to get her to talk about herself and used to look at me with a sort of—well, perhaps hatred is too strong a word for it, yet there was a kind of venom in it. The funny thing was, she liked Hubert much better than she did me, and he didn't like her at all."

"Perhaps she was just a girl who liked men better than women," I said. "Age notwithstanding. She seems to have got on very well with her father when she'd a chance to see him. He said she was gay and warm and forthcoming."

Ann gave a weary shake of her head. "She wasn't. She just thought it worth her while to fool him."

"Well, would you like me to stay on here till Hubert gets back?" I asked. "Or are we in the way? Shall I take Felix home?"

"Don't stay on my account," she answered. "I'm all right. Anyway, I expect Tim and Barbie will stay. But I'm all right. In fact—isn't it awful?—in fact, when all this is over I may be thankful in a dreadful kind of way that something of the sort happened. I don't actually mean that she was murdered—no, I'm not as bad as that—but that the whole thing came to an end, that we're free of her, and without our having had to do anything about it. It was just taken out of our hands. No more arguing with Hubert, no trying to keep up a pretence that I was right when I knew I was wrong. It may even have helped to bring Hubert and me together a little, because of course he'll be sorry for me for a time and he'll be very sweet and gentle. He can be, you know, though usually he doesn't seem to think it's worth the trouble. Oh God, I don't know why I'm running on like this. I'm very fond of Hubert, though I ought never to have married him. I oughtn't to have married anyone. I often envy you, living alone. But I'm sure there are lots of things you want to do now, so I should take Felix home."

I turned towards the door, but then I paused.

"Ann, what do you think Roper meant when he said that there are certain circumstances in the case that are difficult to explain?"

"He could have meant anything," she said. "Or perhaps nothing. Perhaps it was just the fact that she wasn't raped. But that kind of murder sometimes happens without there being an actual rape, doesn't it? I mean, if the man's impotent, or some kind of pervert or something."

"Yes," I said, "I suppose he could have meant that."

She turned again to look at me. "Why do you think he didn't?"

"I don't know. I haven't really thought about it. Perhaps he did."

"What else could he have meant?"

"Nothing that I can think of, unless it could be something to do with the motive for the murder. Suppose they've some evidence they haven't told us about. But if they have, they'll tell Hubert, so you'll hear about it quite soon. Let me know if there's anything I can do for you, won't you? I'll be going now."

I left her, a fragile, stooping figure, seeming almost to be trying to inflict misery on herself in punishment for some strange misdeed, rather than to be feeling any pity for the dead girl. I went downstairs to collect Felix.

As he limped out slowly to the car I thought that the expression on his face was not only one of shock and distress, but also of disgust. He looked positively surly, which was so unlike him that as we started home I said, "Well, you were right from the beginning. It's murder."

He muttered something in reply which I did not catch.

I asked, "What did you say?"

"I said, 'Pompous bloody bastard.' "

"Who? Hubert?" I said. "He's a bit pompous, but he's not as bad as all that."

"No, no, the other chap, Ilsley." He spat the name out as if he found it offensive.

"What's the matter with him?" I said. "I rather liked him."

"You would," he said contemptuously. "Headmaster. Headmaster of some bloody school he started himself where he makes a lot of poor innocents miserable and doesn't do the first thing to equip them for this bloody thing we call life."

"Whatever has got into you?" I asked. "You don't usually throw bloodies around like that."

"Well, it's how I feel. It's how he affected me."

We had reached the gate and turned into the main road. A light rain had started to fall and the morning felt uncomfortably cold. I switched on the windscreen wipers and as they swung backwards and forwards I had a hypnotized feeling of unreality. I felt as if nothing that we had gone through that morning had really happened.

"Why?" I asked.

"Oh, I can tell you why," Felix said. "It's because he reminds me of my own headmaster. Now he was a pompous bloody bastard if there ever was one. Full of good works and high ideals, prayers every morning whether you believed in them or not, and a sadistic bully if ever you found yourself alone in his clutches."

"But I don't think Mr. Ilsley's at all like that," I said. "Whatever makes you think he is?"

Felix passed a hand across his forehead and after a moment seemed to come back from a long way off. He turned his head and smiled at me.

"I honestly don't know," he said. "But for some reason for the last day or two I've been thinking a lot about my school-days. I don't know why. Normally I'm only too glad they were over long ago. A terrible thing, childhood and adolescence. I don't know how one actually survives it. And there are those abominable people who tell one it's the happiest time of one's life. Think of a poor kid looking forward and thinking things are only going to get worse and worse. Did I ever tell you I once tried to cut my throat in one of the school lavatories?"

"No, and I don't believe you ever did," I said. "Probably it was some other poor child who did it and you've only thought of it just this minute. Felix, I want to do a little shopping at the supermarket before we go home. They've a car park. I'll leave you there while I go in and pick up a few things. I shan't be long."

"All right," he said. "But why don't you believe what I told you?"

"Because your sense of self-preservation is much too strong," I said. "Besides, if you'd ever done anything so dramatic you'd have told me about it long ago."

Yet I was not sure that I was right about that. I had been involved myself with Felix in one or two events that were fairly dramatic, yet he hardly ever spoke of them. Reality had very little interest for him. Actually the fact that he had never mentioned a blundering attempt at suicide could just mean that it had happened.

"Talking of cutting throats..." he said.

"Don't!" I said violently.

"But you'll have to face it, you know. And the fact is I've done a most godawful stupid thing."

"What's that?" I asked as I turned the car into the car park beside the supermarket.

"I've left my fingerprints on that knife of Hubert's. I told you how I was fooling with it the other day, didn't I?"

"For heaven's sake, what does that matter?"

"Well, that girl had her throat cut, didn't she?"

I stared at him in astonishment at what he seemed to be suggesting.

"Oh God, what wouldn't I give for a husband without an imagination!" I exclaimed as I opened the door of the car. "And a very nasty imagination at that!"

"Just wait a moment, Virginia," Felix said. "Let me explain. The police are going to be looking for a weapon, aren't they? And that knife would be perfect for the job. It's cut a good many throats already, if Hubert's to be believed. And I told you how I picked it up and handled it, so I've left a perfect set of my fingerprints on it. But the knife that was really used for the job, wherever it is now, will have been wiped clean or will have a whole mixture of prints on it that can quite legitimately be there. So even if it's ever found, it won't tell anyone anything. But there's that one in Hubert's study that will lead straight to me."

"You're contradicting yourself," I said. "If you'd used it for a murder, you'd have wiped it clean yourself. And how do you know it hasn't got Hubert's prints on it, and perhaps Maria Santos's as well, and perhaps even Ann's. Now I want to buy some eggs and some butter and some onions and some of their quiche for lunch—it isn't bad—Oh, and I'd better get some whiskey. I shan't be long."

As I clambered out of the car into the thin rain, Felix muttered, "You drink too much. But while you're at it, you might get me some cigarettes."

Slamming the door shut, I ran to the entrance of the supermarket.

I bought all the things I wanted and though I did it reluctantly I bought a packet of cigarettes for Felix. Doing that, I had the uncomfortable feeling that I was pandering to a dangerous vice. I really did not want Felix to die unnecessarily young of lung cancer or heart disease, yet I had never had the strength of mind to argue the matter out with him. Sometimes I wondered if the stubbornness with which he stuck to smoking when he was quite intelligent enough to understand its hazards, indicated that he himself would not mind dying young. He had not made much of a success of his life and there were times when he seemed to find it almost too tedious and disappointing to be borne. Yet what I had said to him about his sense of self-preservation was true. So I supposed he simply assumed that disasters could only happen to other people.

Emerging from the supermarket, I went to the car and found that Clyde Crendon was sitting on the back seat, behind Felix. I was startled by the pallor of his face. It usually looked so pink and wholesome, but there was no colour in it now and as I opened the car door and dumped my purchases on the seat beside him, he gave me a wild glare that made his plump, pleasant face look frozen with shock.

"Is this true, Virginia?" he asked in a hoarse croak. "I mean, is the girl really dead?"

I slid into the driving seat and pulled the door shut behind me.

"That's what the police have told us," I said.

"Her throat cut?"

"So they said."

"A girl I was talking to only a little while ago! God, how horrible!"

"It is, rather," I agreed.

"I'd been doing some shopping, you see," he went on, "and I came out and I saw Felix sitting here, so I came over to chat, and he told me...He told me...No, I said to myself, it can't be true. But I knew it was true, only I just couldn't take it in that it could happen to someone I knew. I'm sorry I'm such a fool. One hears about that sort of thing happening every other day on television, but it doesn't seem to mean the same then, although it's really just as horrible."

"What Clyde needs is a drink," Felix said. "Let's go to the Rose and Crown."

I thought myself that that was a good idea, so instead of driving home I drove to the old pub in the market square, managed to find some room in the car park behind it, and the three of us went into the bar.

The first thing I saw as we went in was the two men whom I had seen there once before, the big man with the heavy shoulders and the tight brown suit and cheeks as badly shaven as when I had seen him last, and the smaller man with the upstanding hair and the strange, lashless eyes. They were sitting on stools at the bar and saw us come in and immediately looked at one another as if they were consulting on whether or not it was time for them to leave. But without exchanging a word they seemed to come to the conclusion that they should stay, though they turned their backs very deliberately on the room, putting their elbows on the counter and pushing their beer mugs forward for more drinks.

Felix hobbled to one of the small round tables and dropped into a chair there, grimacing as if his leg was hurting him, but at the same time he gave the two men a thoughtful look, certainly recognizing them. The barman brought us our drinks at the table. Clyde gulped eagerly at his.

"What a fool you must think me," he said. "Just give me a minute or two and I'll calm down. I expect you think it's really very funny that someone who writes the sort of books I do should be so squeamish, but I've always been terribly squeamish, terribly. I'll tell you a ridiculous thing that happened to me once. I was at a lecture being given by one of those forensic science chaps and he was showing slides to illustrate the lecture. And, one of the slides was of a girl who'd been raped and battered to death and he left it on the screen for some minutes and went on chatting cheerfully about it and all of a sudden I fainted. Crazy, wasn't it? I mean, it was only a picture. But that was the trouble—*seeing* it, you see—that's what I found so upsetting. I could have described the same thing in detail in my own words and not felt a thing, but seeing it—that was altogether different."

"I know what you mean," Felix said, but he said it absently, his gaze still on the two men at the bar.

As if they felt it on the backs of their necks, they both suddenly got off their stools, turned, and came towards our table.

"Hi," the smaller one said to Felix. He seemed to be the more articulate of the two.

"Hallo," Felix answered.

"Seen you somewhere, haven't I?" the small man said.

"I saw you in here a few days ago," Felix replied.

"That's not what I mean. In London. I know, the Fox and Grapes. Isn't that so?"

"It could be," Felix said coolly, apparently not in a mood to encourage familiarity.

"That's right, that's where it was," the small man asserted. "What are you doing here now?"

"It seems to me that's my own business."

"All right, all right. No offence. All the same, what are you doing here?"

"I'm convalescing in the house of a friend after a very painful accident. Does that satisfy you?"

"I can see you been in an accident," the small man said impatiently, looking at the plaster on Felix's leg. "But why come *here*, that's what I'd like to know."

"Because it happens to be where my friend lives."

The small man looked at Clyde Crendon.

"You his friend? You know him then?"

"I don't understand," Clyde said unhappily. "What's this all about? No, we're friends, but Mr. Freer isn't staying with me."

"He's staying with me," I said. "Time was when we were married, though I can't see what that's got to do with you." The man's eyes, with their naked, peering stare, worried me. "What I'd like to know is what you're doing here."

"Oh, you would, would you? Well, I'll tell you, my dear. My brother and I come down here for a bit of peace and quiet. That's all we want and it's not much to ask, is it? My brother hasn't been well and he needs a holiday. But here's our Mr. Freer who I distinctly remember I had a long talk with over a few drinks in the Fox and Grapes, so he needn't say he doesn't know me. Here he is, I say, following us about and probably stirring up trouble for us, because we've both had our troubles in our time, when all we want is peace and quiet." He turned again to Clyde. "You know the sort he is, do you? You know you can't trust him as far as you can see him."

"That's needlessly insulting," Felix said. "And I haven't been wasting my time following you, any more than I expect you've been following me. Or have you been following me? Have you some peculiar interest in my movements? If you have, I'd very much like to know the reason for it."

"There's nothing peculiar about me or my interests," the small man said indignantly. "But you've been working in that house the girl disappeared from, haven't you? Kidnapped, isn't that what they're saying? I can't understand about that. I shouldn't have thought it was in your line, kidnapping. But then again, perhaps it is. People like you, one doesn't know where one is with you. The question is, do I tell this gentleman you're not quite what you seem? That's just what I might do if me and my brother find you're taking an interest in us."

The big man suddenly put a hand on the other's shoulder.

"Come along," he muttered in a low, rumbling voice. "You won't get anywhere with him."

He seemed almost to pick the small man up, turn him around, and thrust him ahead of him to the door.

"I don't understand," Clyde said again in a tone of distress. "Do you really know them, Felix? That man was very rude."

"Yes, he was, wasn't he?" Felix agreed, but once more in an absent way with his thoughts plainly on something else. After a moment he went on, "Everyone seems to know about the kidnapping, but the police are still keeping quiet about the murder. I wonder when they'll let it out."

"But those two men," Clyde said, "who are they? What do you really think they were doing here?"

"I don't know. But I expect you'd like to ask me what they meant when they said I'm not what I seem," Felix remarked.

"No, no, of course not," Clyde said hurriedly. "He was just being offensive. That was obvious. But they're afraid of you for some reason. I was wondering why."

"It's just that they know I'll guess they're up to no good. I do happen to know that the big man's just out of gaol and the younger one's done time on various occasions. They're a couple of moderately successful burglars, I believe. I wonder how genuinely they think I've been following them around. As if one could do such a thing with a great chunk of plaster on one's leg. But if they don't think so, why should they make that scene?"

"Guilty consciences," Clyde said. "A feeling that everyone's against them. I think I'd like another drink. What about you?"

He bought drinks for the three of us and when he returned to the table with them lapsed into thoughtful silence. He seemed calmer than he had been earlier, less distraught, as if he were getting used to the idea that someone whom he had had to lunch in his home only a week ago had been horribly murdered.

❉ ❉ ❉

Felix had a frown on his face and was brooding, I thought, on our encounter with the two men. Fairly soon I suggested that I should drive Clyde home before Felix and I made for home ourselves, but Clyde said that he would sooner walk. When we left the Rose and Crown he set off briskly along the street, walking vigorously, as though he had dropped some burden of which he was glad to be free.

"Funny," Felix observed as I started the car and drove out of the car park, "the way he went to pieces when I told him about the murder. Didn't it strike you as odd?"

"Because of the sort of thing he writes, d'you mean?" I said. "I've never thought thrillers and detective stories, or whatever you like to call them, have anything to do with real crime. For that you've got to go to Sophocles, Shakespeare, and those people. Clyde's books are just excellent bedtime reading."

"No, I didn't mean that," Felix said. "I'd have found his reaction a bit excessive even if all he ever wrote were nice little stories about fairies and flowers for three-year-old children. I couldn't help wondering if it was real."

I was puzzled. "Why shouldn't it be? Why should he put it on?"

"I don't know. But, as I said, I can't help wondering about it, just as I wondered about what he really wanted with us yesterday evening."

"I think it was real today," I said. "I remember his face when I came out of the supermarket and saw him with you in the car. It was chalk white and that's a thing you can't put on. I believe some people can weep to order, but I don't think anyone can suddenly go pale as death, or blush either, unless there's a real emotion at work. Anyway, why should he pretend to be more upset than he was? I think he's just a very sensitive little man who'd convinced himself he was just the tiniest bit in love with Holly."

Felix was gazing dreamily before him. He murmured, " 'I met Murder in the way—He had a mask like Castlereagh...' Who said that?"

"Shelley, I believe," I answered.

"I wonder what Castlereagh had done to annoy him so. And I wonder what his face was like. History isn't my strong point. But I think you're right, though it hadn't occurred to me before. One can mask one's real feelings with smiles and frowns and even tears, but I don't believe one can change colour. So poor Clyde really was upset and you think he was falling for Holly. What do you think she felt about him?"

"I never saw any sign of her feeling anything about anybody." We had reached my gate and I stopped the car. Getting out of it, I went round it to help Felix out. "I'll put the quiche in the oven. It won't take long to warm up."

I picked up the things that I had bought in the supermarket and led the way to the front door.

We had the *quiche* about twenty minutes later and then some coffee. Then Felix settled himself on the sofa and a few minutes later was fast asleep. I thought of telephoning Ann to ask if Hubert had returned yet, but decided against it. He would probably not be home for at least a couple of hours. Even when he got there it was unlikely that he would have anything special to say, unless he could explain what Inspector Roper had meant when he spoke of circumstances in the case which it was difficult to understand.

The only thing that I could think of that needed explaining was why Holly's body had been taken so far away instead of being dumped in some pond or wood nearer to Allingford, where she had obviously been picked up. There must be plenty of suitable places quite near. Had it been done in the hope that she would not be identified and the connection with Allingford not be discovered? It seemed probable enough and, apart from that, the crime seemed to follow lines that have become only too drearily familiar to those of us who watch television.

Picking up *The Times*, I started idly reading it, then remembered suddenly how I had seen the notice of Sara Noble's death.

"...peacefully at her home..."

Though her death had been peaceful, it seemed to me now to have been the beginning of all the distress that had followed. Before it life had been normal, quiet, uneventful, but only a short time after I had read the obituary Ann had rung up to tell me about the sale of the Baraud picture at Christie's, and ever since then I seemed to have become involved in the Brightwells' lives in a way that I never had before. And Felix had arrived and I had met Clyde Crendon and the two burglars too, if that was what they were...

I am not sure how long it was before the paper slipped out of my hands and like Felix I fell into a doze.

It was Felix who woke me presently by suddenly exclaiming, "A woman like Sara Noble! Whatever did she see in him?"

This was so close to what I had been thinking about myself before dropping off to sleep that I wondered for a moment if it was I who had said it. But Felix was wide awake now, smoking a cigarette as usual, and, when he was certain that I was awake, almost repeated his question. "A woman like Sara Noble, successful, talented, beautiful—what got her involved with a pompous nonentity like Ilsley?"

"I think he was probably very good-looking when he was young," I said. "And he may have been a nice change after the kind of people she met in the theatre. And I don't see why you should hold it against him so much that he reminds you of your own headmaster. That isn't his fault."

"I'm not so sure about that," he said darkly. "All that gang have something in common. But it's a funny thing how I keep thinking about that miserable school I went to. You know, if it hadn't been the kind of place it was, my whole life might have been different. Have you ever noticed that I've a certain natural aptitude for mathematics?"

"I've noticed you seem to have a natural aptitude for making the pounds you owe people turn into pence, if not to disappear altogether," I said, "and the pence they owe you turn into pounds."

"That's got nothing to do with mathematics," he said irritably. "The fact is, I had a natural gift for it, but that unspeakable headmaster of ours taught maths himself and so sickened me of the whole subject that I left school at the first moment I could and got a job digging drains for the council. And from that, as you know, I graduated slowly and painfully to selling secondhand cars. If it hadn't been for him I'd have stayed on and got my G.C.E. and gone on to a university and would probably be an expert on computers by now and making lots of money. Would you have stayed with me if I'd been able to make lots of money, Virginia?"

"The question is academic," I said.

"You mean, I'd have been a different person, don't you? But in that case, you might have stayed. Or perhaps not. Perhaps you'd never have fallen in love with me, even for a little while. Aren't these sort of questions fascinating? All the things that might have happened, or not happened, if everything had been different. But did I ever tell you about my great mathematical success when I was at school?"

"I don't believe so," I replied.

"Mathematical and financial," he said. "The fact is, I could cope with the homework we had to do much more easily than most of the other kids, and I started a nice little racket, getting through it quickly, then handing on the results to anyone else who wanted them for a bob a time. I made as much as a quid on some days. But unfortunately it didn't last long. One evening I must have been tired or worried or something, because I made two mistakes in my work. And next day, of course, half the class had exactly the same two mistakes in their work. So I was unmasked, and instead of being praised for intelligence and enterprise, I got a beating from that foul character who was teaching us, and what specially hurt, he made me hand over all my profits for that day to him. And I bet he just pocketed it and spent it on a bottle of gin or some such thing. And that's what really decided my future. I wasn't going to go on working under a crook like him."

"Felix," I said, "you've always told me you were at a public school."

"That's right. A very minor one, but still I had the so-called education of an English gentleman—ha, ha!"

"A boarding school?"

"Of course. Rife with sexual perversion and with totally unheated classrooms. It wasn't until I left school that I discovered that chilblains aren't an inevitable characteristic of an English winter."

"But if you were at a boarding school, how did it come about that you were doing homework? That's what a child takes home to do in the evenings from a day school."

"Did I say homework?" he said. "A slip of the tongue. Of course I meant prep."

I gave a sigh. "I've never believed in that school, you know. I think you were at a secondary modern, as I think it would have been called in those days, though now it would be a comprehensive. The truth is, you're a shocking snob."

"So you don't believe any of what I've been telling you," he said.

"Oh, I believe the story about the homework. That's in character."

"The funny thing is, I don't believe I've thought about it for years. I wonder why it came into my head today. Meeting that man Ilsley, I suppose. I could just see him pocketing the modest profits of some poor hardworking child. But what d'you think he'd spend the money on? A quid wouldn't go far these days."

"It would be more than a quid. The rate for the work would be considerably higher than a shilling. But, Felix, tell me something, you seemed puzzled at the scene those two men made in the Rose and Crown. I thought it was puzzling too. What did you really think it was all about?"

He tipped cigarette ash into the saucer on the floor beside the sofa before he answered, and when he did he sounded hesitant.

"I don't know. I really don't know. The only thing I can think of is so fantastic that it can't be true."

"What is it?"

He shook his head. "No, it isn't possible. If I told you you'd only say it was imagination running away with me. Of course they're up to something and I suppose it's just conceivable that they thought I'd been keeping an eye on them, even with a leg in plaster, and would get them into trouble. Perhaps they'd heard I helped the police a bit over that murder in Little Carberry Street and they think I'm some sort of undercover agent. They aren't particularly intelligent specimens of the human race."

"What do you think they meant when they threatened to tell Clyde that you weren't what you seemed?"

"I didn't think they really meant anything in particular. Unless, of course—no, that's fantastic too. I think it was just an idle threat."

I would have liked very much to find out what it had been about the behaviour of the two men in the pub which seemed to Felix so fantastic, because he has a way of taking very fantastic things for granted, but before I could ask him another question the doorbell rang.

With a sense of deep depression I assumed that it was the police again. I did not know of anyone else who was likely to call that day. As it turned out, I was wrong, but the depression did not lessen when I opened the door and saw who was there. It was Hubert and Lionel Ilsley and the grave expressions on both their faces told me that almost for certain they were bringing bad news.

"I'm sorry to trouble you, Virginia," Hubert said, "but we've come to you for help. A very shocking thing has happened and I'm scared of the effect it may have on Ann. I thought if you would come home with us and be there when we break the news, it might, so to speak, soften the blow."

"I'll do anything I can," I said. "But come in and tell me what it is."

In my own ears I sounded calm, but I could tell that in a grim kind of way both men were frightened, and their fear, or perhaps it was really horror, communicated itself to me and sent a chill through me that seemed to get into my bones. I led them into the sitting room.

Felix got clumsily to his feet, but neither Hubert nor Lionel Ilsley did more than give him a brief nod. Then they both looked at me again.

"We asked the police to drop us here instead of taking us straight home," Hubert said, "because I wanted to have this talk with you. They've just driven us back from East Wellfleet, where we saw the girl's body."

"And it's Holly?" I said. "There isn't any doubt of it?"

"None at all," Hubert answered. "Apart from the finger-prints the police have got, Ilsley identified her. He knew her at once. No, there's no doubt it's Holly Noble. But she isn't the girl who's been living with us here. She doesn't in the least resemble her. And the police told us she's been dead for about a fortnight."

# Chapter Seven

"So that's what they meant by circumstances that it was difficult to explain," Felix said. "That she'd been dead for so long when they'd been told she was alive here."

Hubert nodded. "Yes, that was it."

"But then the girl who was here—who is she?" I asked.

"We don't know."

"And what was she doing here?"

"There are various possibilities," Hubert said. "But she was introduced into our house at just about the time the real Holly was murdered, so at least it's probable the two events are connected."

"And what's happened to her now?" I said. "Where is she?"

"Personally, I don't give a damn," Hubert answered. "She was up to no good and I'll be glad if we never see her again. But will you come with us, Virginia, and help us tell Ann what's happened? I've been worried about her ever since that girl disappeared. She's taken it very hard. She'd got really fond of her and it's going to be a nasty blow to find she was being deceived. She was just being used in some way. And I'm afraid of being clumsy in the way I tell her about it. I'm generally clumsy about anything like that. Not that anything like it has ever happened to us before, but I mean about breaking bad news and so on."

Remembering my talk with Ann, I thought he had less need to be afraid of the effect of his news on her than he thought, but I supposed he was the sort of man who all his life had been afraid of the emotions of women and who had never even begun to understand them. He expected to have to face a hysterical scene and wanted me to help him get through it.

I said that of course I would go with him, if that was what he wanted, then I discovered that although he had not been invited, Felix had every intention of accompanying us. I realized that he was eaten up with curiosity about the whole affair and that it would be very difficult to persuade him to stay behind, even if that had been what it would have been proper for him to do.

But in a way I was glad to have him with us. He is observant, shrewd, and much cleverer than I am at fathoming the motives of other people, particularly if these are rather disreputable. If it should turn out to be possible to guess at what the false Holly had been doing in the Brightwells' house, he was the likeliest person of all those who had been in contact with her to arrive at it.

The four of us got into my car.

As we started, Lionel Ilsley said, "You know, in some way I'm not surprised at what's happened. When we were talking about Holly this morning, when Lady Brightwell said how shy and reserved she was and I told you how cheerful and friendly everyone normally found her, I almost felt we were talking about two different people. And that's how it's turned out. But perhaps that's only hindsight."

"You can hardly wonder at her being reserved," Hubert said bitterly. "Downright secretive, I used to think it. But that's easy to understand now. If she only knew a few things about your daughter, she'd have been very careful what she said about her friends and her school and her background. And probably she wouldn't play her violin to us because she couldn't play at all."

"I wonder how the substitution was made," Lionel Ilsley said. "Someone must have met Holly when she got back from Rome, or perhaps even before she left it, and persuaded her to go with him to the place, wherever it was, that he killed her, while the other girl came out of the plane and, as you told me, was met by Lady Brightwell. I suppose the police will find it out in time."

"They'll find it out quickly enough when they catch up with that wretched girl we've been entertaining," Hubert said.

"If they ever do," Felix said.

The remark somehow silenced the other two men as if for the first time it had just occurred to them that conceivably the shy, reserved impostor who had vanished might be dead too by now.

When we reached the Brightwells' house we found Ann in the drawing room, her face drawn but without any sign of the tears on it that I had seen streaming down her cheeks when I had last been with her. Tim and Barbie were there and so was Clyde Crendon.

I wondered what he was doing there and whether he had come straight away instead of going home when he left the Rose and Crown. If he had, and if for some reason he had not wanted Felix and me to know that that was what he intended, it would explain why he had refused the lift in my car that I had offered him. But why should he mind about our knowing?

He was looking restless and nervous and as if he could hardly wait for the news that Hubert and Lionel Ilsley were bringing, while Tim and Barbie, whose features were very dissimilar yet whose expressions just then were strangely alike, apprehensive yet carefully under control, seemed very still and quiet.

Ann jumped to her feet as we came in.

"Well?" she said, her soft voice almost harsh for once. "Was it Holly?"

Hubert looked helplessly at me and waited for me to answer.

Before I could do so, Clyde exclaimed, "It can't be—surely it can't be!" He was almost wringing his plump hands.

Ann made an impatient gesture to silence him. "Is it?"

"I can only tell you what Hubert's told me," I said. "Yes, it's Holly. But it isn't the girl who's been staying here."

Thinking how craven Hubert was to leave the telling of the story to me, I went on and told Ann as much of it as I knew from him. All the time that I was talking she kept her eyes on his face. There was a touch of contempt in them as if she too thought that by bringing me into it he was showing himself cowardly. But she took the news calmly.

Turning to Lionel Ilsley, she said, "I'm sorry, so very sorry, for you, Mr. Ilsley. It must have been a terrible shock."

He nodded gravely, "It was. But, remember, I was expecting it to be Holly. The worst shock came when the police came here and told us she was dead. They didn't mention then how long she'd been dead, so I'd no reason to think she wasn't the girl who'd been staying with you."

"Of course, I always knew there was something wrong with her—with that girl, I mean, whoever she is," Ann said. "At first I thought it must be my fault, but then I began to have suspicions…"

She was interrupted at that moment by the fact that Clyde Crendon had just crumpled up gently on the floor in a dead faint.

Barbie gave a cry and looked as if she might be going to faint too. Hubert and Tim sprang forward, stooping to take hold of Clyde and heave him onto the sofa. At that point I interfered, having, I supposed, slightly more experience of such things than they had. Advising them to leave him where he was, I said, "He'll be all right in a minute or two. I believe he's rather given to fainting. Only this morning he was telling Felix and me how he fainted in a lecture when he saw a rather gruesome slide on the screen." I put a cushion under his head. "There, I think he's coming to already."

His eyelids had fluttered and after only a moment his eyes opened and he looked at us confusedly. His face was very white and his body seemed limp.

"What happened?" he asked in a half-whispering voice. "Oh, I know, I passed out. I'm sorry, I'm terribly sorry. I'd better go home and get out of your way. I'm terribly sorry. Please don't worry about it. It's just that I'm stupid about some things—always have been. I'll go home."

"I think you'd better have a bit of a lie-down first," Ann said. "Just for a little while. Tim, help him onto the sofa."

"But I don't want to be a nuisance," Clyde protested. "I'm quite all right now."

Tim was helping him to his feet. Clyde sat down heavily on the sofa and leant forward, taking his head in his hands.

"No hurry," Hubert said. Having in his time, according to himself, cut a number of throats and never been unduly upset by it, he seemed to find Clyde's behaviour embarrassing rather than anything else.

"I suppose you haven't had a telephone call from the kidnappers?" he asked Ann.

"No, there's been nothing," she answered.

"I wonder if they know they've got the wrong girl," he said. "They could have been deceived about her just as we were and believed she was really Holly Noble. Or if they knew she'd been murdered, they could have sent this other girl in her place to cooperate in a fake kidnapping. Roper didn't tell me what the police think."

"They can't have much to go on yet," Tim said.

Clyde had staggered to his feet.

"Really, I must go home now," he said. "You've been so kind to me, I'm very grateful, and I'm so sorry I was such a fool. Ridiculous, wasn't it? But I don't want to go on being a nuisance. But if you'd just let me know—no, that's troubling you. I won't bother you."

"What is it?" Ann asked.

"It's only that I can't help feeling I'd like to know what you hear from the kidnappers. But please don't bother about it. Only, you see, I feel I'm involved in this somehow. Not that I really am, I suppose, apart from having heard about it. All the same, if you should hear anything…" He left the sentence unfinished.

"I'll see you home," Tim said. "You look a bit shaky."

"No, no, I'm perfectly all right. Thank you, thank you. And again, my apologies."

Clyde made his way to the door.

It was only then, as I looked after him, that I realized that Felix was not in the room. During the commotion that had followed Clyde's collapse, he had quietly slipped out.

It worried me, because although I guessed that he had only gone to Hubert's study, which so far as I knew was the only room in the house, besides the drawing room and the dining room, with which he was familiar, I could not think why he should have gone out just at a time when the normal thing surely, would have been to show concern for Clyde. I hesitated for a moment, then decided to go and look for him.

I went out into the hall and as I did so saw Felix come out of Hubert's study, At that same moment the Baraud painting, *Le Repas en plein* air, happened to catch my eye and I stopped in front of it.

I did not know why I did so. I had seen it often and sometimes I had stood still to look at it, as I did now, enjoying the sense of brightness and quiet and intimacy that the Victorian ladies and gentlemen in it gave me, and sometimes I passed it by without a thought, treating it as an unimportant part of the furnishing of the hall. At the moment it might have been the sheer contrast between it and everything else that had been happening in the house that held me. I did not move when Felix came and stood beside me.

I said, "Did you know that Degas once said a painting requires as much cunning as the perpetration of a crime?"

"Who told you that?" Felix asked.

"Clyde, the first time I met him."

"Well, I should think the converse is true, that the perpetration of a crime takes as much cunning as a painting. Artistry, you know, composition, planning. As you know, I'm not up in the arts and of course it wouldn't apply if the crime was just something sudden and crude. But I don't feel that's what these people here are up against."

"Felix, what were you doing in Hubert's study?"

"Oh, just tidying up some papers," he said. "I'm going to tell him I'm giving up the job, but I thought I ought to leave things in order."

"It didn't seem to take you long."

"No. Well, they were pretty well sorted out already. I was only checking a few things."

We went into the drawing room.

As we did so the telephone started to ring.

Hubert picked it up swiftly and announced that it was Hubert Brightwell speaking. Then he said, "Oh...Ah yes...Yes, I see...No, nothing..."

After that I could hear the clucking of a voice in the telephone that he held to his ear that went on for some time. His face became stern as he listened and his lips tightened. Everyone else in the room became silent. It struck me too that we had all suddenly become immobile, holding ourselves in rigidly motionless attitudes. Lionel Ilsley had just taken a handkerchief out of his pocket but seemed to have nothing to do with it. Barbie had a hand on Tim's shoulder and it seemed to tighten there as if it could not let go. Even Felix, with a cigarette halfway to his mouth, held it stationary instead of lighting it. Ann had sat down abruptly in the nearest chair and was holding her head in her hands.

At last Hubert said, "Yes, of course, I understand. Yes, certainly. Thank you."

That did not sound like the way he would terminate a conversation with kidnappers.

As he put the telephone down Ann said, "Then it wasn't them? It wasn't instructions?"

"No, it was Roper again," Hubert said. "He was asking me if we'd had any instructions yet, then he told me that we should all be very careful not to mention the murder of Holly

Noble to anyone until he gives us permission. Particularly not to the press. The point is that if the kidnappers of the girl who stayed with us still believe she's Holly, in other words that they had nothing to do with the murder, they may still be caught. It's a matter of some importance what's actually happened to that girl."

"I don't care what's happened to her!" Ann exclaimed. "I don't care if she's been murdered too!"

Hubert looked startled but went to her and gave her one of his clumsy caresses. "You don't mean that. Of course you don't. But the fact is, we've got to go on waiting for instructions, and as soon as we've got them we're to get in touch with the police."

"But we aren't going to pay anything to anybody," Ann said.

"Of course not. All the same, though the girl got herself into this household on false pretences—why, we don't know— kidnapping her is a crime. And even if it isn't a real kidnapping, but just an attempt she's in on herself to extort money from us, that's a crime too. So we want whoever is at the back of it caught and we'll do what the police want. We won't speak about the murder to anyone." He looked round the room. "Understood?"

We all murmured that we understood. Then movement returned to the room. Lionel Ilsley blew his nose. Felix lit his cigarette. Barbie released Tim, and Ann sat back in her chair, letting her hands fall into her lap.

I said, "Felix, I think it's time we went home."

He started and said, "Oh…Oh yes, of course. There's just something I wanted to say." He turned to Hubert. "I think you've realized I'm not qualified to be much help to you with your book. It was Tim's idea that I might be. He knew I was looking for a temporary job and he wanted to help me out. But the work's turned out to be far more difficult than I thought it would be and I'm afraid I've let you down. So I thought I'd go home tomorrow, if that's convenient for you. I've just been into the study and made sure the papers we've already worked on are in order. Perhaps you'd like to check them before I go."

"Well, if that's how you feel…" Hubert began, but paused then, looking uncertain. "I don't want you to think I've been dissatisfied, Felix. The fact is, the job's more difficult than I thought myself it would be. I've always been able to chat about the things that have happened to me and I've really had a very interesting life. But it's turned out harder than I thought it would be to get it all down on paper. And with what's been happening during the last day or two, it's been hard to concentrate." He hesitated again. "All right then, we'll call it off for the present."

He meant that he would call it off for good. The departure of Felix, together with the kidnapping and the murder and having police in and out of the house, gave him an excellent alibi for dropping the work altogether, which he was grateful for, since he had not derived the satisfaction from it that he had expected. I doubted if the matter would ever be raised again, except in the form of something that he would still get down to sometime or other, when he had the time.

"If you'd just take a look at the way I've left things, before I go," Felix said, "I'd feel easier in my mind."

"No need for that, I'm sure," Hubert replied.

"All the same, if you wouldn't mind…"

I was puzzled by Felix's insistence. It was not in character for him to be particularly solicitous about how he had left a jumble of papers, and whenever he did something that was markedly out of character I always felt uneasily that there was probably some motive behind it which would not bear examination.

But Hubert shrugged his shoulders and said, "All right, if that's what you want."

He left the room.

Tim seemed to be thinking much as I was about the future of Hubert's autobiography, for he gave one of his sardonic smiles and said, "I'm sorry, Felix, I seem to have got you into a mess. However, between us I should think we've managed to cure my uncle of his literary ambitions. As a matter of fact, I always knew they'd come to nothing and I didn't think you'd be very efficient as a ghost, but I thought the arrangement would last longer than it has and would help you through this time when you can't get around properly. But I didn't make allowances for crime. Are you really going back to London tomorrow?"

I wanted to tell Felix that there was no need for him to go if he did not really want to, but thought that that could wait till we were alone.

Barbie had gone to Ann and was sitting on the arm of her chair and had put an arm round her shoulders.

"Cheer up, darling," she said. "Things will sort themselves out somehow."

"Why don't those instructions come?" Ann asked shrilly. "How much longer are they going to keep us waiting?"

"Does it matter so much now?" Barbie asked. "However Holly got herself murdered, it had nothing to do with you. And you know you aren't going to pay up for the other girl, so I'd stop worrying about the instructions, even if the police do want to know about them."

Hubert came striding back into the room. His face was red with anger.

"My knife!" he shouted. "It's gone! What's happened to it? You—" He turned on Felix. "You knew about this, didn't you? That's why you wanted me to go in there. What's happened to it?"

### ❃ ❃ ❃

"Your knife?" Felix sounded bewildered, but his face looked particularly bland, which made me feel fairly sure he was about to tell a lie. However, it was not exactly a lie that he told, except by implication. It was an innocent-sounding question that he asked.

"What knife?"

"The one on my desk," Hubert bellowed at him. "The one I caught you fooling with the other day. I told you it was a souvenir of my war days and I didn't want you touching it. Where is it?"

Felix gave a helpless little shake of his head.

"I don't know anything about it."

"But you've been in the room," Hubert said. "You told me so yourself."

"But I wasn't thinking about the knife. I didn't notice it was missing."

Hubert looked round at the rest of us.

"Who else has been in there?"

No one answered.

Then Ann said impatiently, "If you're talking about that horrible dagger of yours, I'm glad if it's gone. I've always hated it."

"It meant a lot to me," Hubert said, "and it's missing."

"It'll turn up somewhere," she said. "Things nearly always do. You think they've been lost or stolen and you go nearly out of your mind, looking for them, then you find they've fallen behind a bookcase, or perhaps you've taken them upstairs to do some odd job and left them up there and forgotten about it."

"I did not take my knife upstairs to do any job whatever!" Hubert said furiously. "And I looked behind the bookcase and under the bureau and in its drawers and it's not there."

"Perhaps Santos borrowed it," Tim suggested. "He may have been short of a sharp knife in the kitchen and thought it was just the thing he needed to slice up some steak or something."

"Don't make me sick!" Ann exploded. "Hubert's cut *throats* with that knife. If Santos has really taken it to cut up some meat for dinner tonight, I shan't be able to touch it."

"All the same, that's a good idea of Tim's," Hubert said. "I think I'll go and ask Santos if he knows anything about it. He'll get a flea in his ear if he's taken it."

He again strode out of the room.

"Well, I think Virginia and I had better leave you now," Felix said, a little obviously seizing the opportunity to get away while Hubert was out of the room. "If you get instructions from any kidnappers, Ann, we'd be glad to hear about them. But that's just curiosity. I know we can't help in any way."

He limped towards the door and, after saying a brief goodbye to Ann and the others, I followed him.

Faint dusk had fallen while we had been in the house and I switched on the lights of the car before starting for home. There was a chill in the early evening which exaggerated a chill I felt in myself, though the house that we had just left had been warm. It was an internal chill, a matter of emotion and nerves, a sensation to which I am liable when I am under stress.

I felt a hurry to get home, to make some tea, to sit on the floor by the fire, to shut Felix out of my thoughts, to convince myself that life was everyday and normal and that no one would ring up to tell us anything more about the fate of the nameless girl who had vanished. For the moment I did not care what had happened to her.

But after a minute or two I said, "Felix, did you take that knife?"

"Me?" Felix said. "Whatever should I do that for?"

"I don't know. I often don't know why you do the things you do." Unthinkingly I touched the necklace of agate beads that he had given me and which he might or might not have paid for. "You do often help yourself to things that take your fancy, don't you?"

He did not bother to deny it, but he shook his head. "Can you imagine me taking a fancy to a knife—to that sort, anyway, that makes you almost automatically think of murder?"

"Then what were you doing in Hubert's study?"

"It's obvious, really. I thought I'd take the opportunity to wipe my prints off that knife. I haven't felt happy, knowing they were there."

"And the knife truly was missing?"

"Yes."

"So you persuaded Hubert to go and take a look in the room to check that you'd left his papers in order, when really you wanted to see if it would worry him that the knife was missing."

"Yes, there was always the chance that he'd removed it himself for some purpose or other."

"Who do you think took it?"

"I haven't any idea."

"And why?"

"That's what worries me," Felix said. "Why? Because someone else thinks his fingerprints may be on it? Because it's already been used in a horrible way? Or because of something he thinks he might do with it?"

I turned that over in my mind before I went on. "You don't seriously think it was used for the murder of Holly Noble, do you? Because if you do…'"

"Well?" he said as I paused.

"No," I said, "that's too ridiculous. Because if it was used for that, there's really no one who could have used it but Hubert. We know from the way he behaved today that if anyone else had taken it and it had been missing for even a little while, he'd have noticed it at once and made a fuss about it."

"And you don't think it could have been Hubert who did it?"

"Of course not. Apart from anything else, why should he?"

"That's something I've been asking myself. Why should he? I rather wish I could answer that, because somehow I like the idea of his turning out to be guilty. He's such a successful, respected man who's never been connected with anything disreputable, the kind I always half-hope will come a cropper. But the trouble is, they mostly don't, they just go on being successful and respected, and quite justifiably too. The only possible reason I can think of why he might have killed Holly is if he'd had a secret love affair with her. If he had, and if he was dead scared of Ann finding out about it, the last thing he'd want would be for Holly to come to live in their house. What do you think of that for a motive?"

"It couldn't be more ridiculous."

"I was afraid you'd say that, though I don't really see why you should. Actually it all fits together rather well. To begin with, he'd have known how to get Holly on the telephone in Rome and could have told her to come on an earlier plane than the one Ann was going to meet, and he could have gone to meet the earlier plane himself and driven off into the country with her, murdered her, and dumped her body in that pond where the boys found her. What's wrong with that? The fuss he made about the knife today may have been because he was afraid someone had caught on to what he'd done. I wonder if he's got an alibi for the day Holly arrived. I'm sure the police will look into that very carefully. You know, you shouldn't assume someone like Hubert is incapable of having a secret love affair. He's probably got as many human failings as most people."

"I don't believe it for a moment," I said. "Leaving his morals out of the question, why should he have provided a substitute Holly for the one he'd killed? Because a girl wearing a white flower came off the plane from Rome and was met by Ann and brought home and has been living in that house until a day or two ago. Why should Hubert have arranged that?"

"Ah," Felix said, sounding pleased, as if I were a bright child in a class he was teaching who had asked an intelligent question, "that's where we get around to a fact I'm sure of, that we're dealing with two criminals. Two crimes. Two unconnected things. Or if they're connected, it's only by the flimsiest of links. Perhaps because someone's made a blunder."

"I don't understand," I said. "What do you mean?"

But before he could answer we had arrived at my gate and, though I sat still in the car for a moment, looking into his face to see if he would reply, he turned to the door beside him, opened it, and began to clamber out. So I got out myself and went round the car to help him, then got back into the car and drove it into the garage.

By the time that I had him on the doorstep, unlocked the door, and the two of us had gone in, I had half-forgotten what my question had been. He had said something about there having been two crimes and I had wanted him to explain it. But I also wanted tea, and as he hobbled into the sitting room I went to the kitchen and put the kettle on. By the time that I carried the tea tray into the sitting room, all I could remember of our talk in the car was his fantastic theory that Hubert might be the murderer of Holly Noble. In a slightly macabre way, I found it funny.

Pouring out the tea, I said, "Are you really going home tomorrow?"

"I think I might as well," he answered.

"Then hadn't you better phone Hermione this evening and ask her to lay in some supplies for you?"

"Perhaps I should."

"You needn't go, you know, unless you want to."

"Would you sooner I didn't?"

"Oh, I didn't mean that. Do as you like."

"I was just wondering if you were finding all this crime a bit much to cope with," he said. "If I'm any kind of support, of course I'll stay on."

The peculiar thing was that I was finding him a support, though I did not want to admit it. Ever since we had separated I had done my best to make no claims on him whatever. He had not been quite so scrupulous about making no claims on me, but on the whole we had managed to maintain a reasonably friendly, unresentful relationship without allowing our lives to become unduly entangled again. But there was no doubt about it at the moment that if he were to go back to London tomorrow I should miss him, though there was something very odd to me about the thought that Felix could ever be a support to anyone.

"I was just thinking about that leg of yours," I said hypocritically. "Do you really think you can manage?"

He gave me one of his most charming smiles and I knew that he had seen through me. However, he answered gravely, "Actually I'm not sure how well I should, though Hermione's a dear girl and would do all she could to help. But I don't really like the thought of leaving you to handle things here by yourself, particularly now that that knife's gone missing."

"Are you suggesting someone's going to murder me?" I asked.

"I should think that's unlikely," he said, "but it's going to be used for something, isn't it?"

I took a moment to digest that, then I said, "If that's what you think, oughtn't we to tell the police it's gone missing?"

"I expect Hubert's done that already. It's for him to do it, isn't it?"

"Perhaps it is."

I was not sure whether or not I thought it was and did not feel altogether happy about leaving things as they were. But in my uncertainty, brooding on the disappearance of the knife, I suddenly remembered the question that I had asked Felix in the car and that he had not answered.

"You haven't told me why you think we're dealing with two criminals," I said. "And what did you mean when you said someone had blundered?"

"Did I say that?" he asked.

"You know you did."

"Well, yes, perhaps. But I'm not sure about anything."

"All the same, tell me what you meant."

He ran his fingers through his hair, looking puzzled, as if he could not remember what he had said to me.

"You see, someone got hold of that girl, Holly Noble," he said, "and got her out of the way and murdered her and planted another girl in the Brightwells' house in her place, didn't they?"

"That's how it looks," I agreed.

"And we don't know why they did that, though I've got some ideas about it. But they're very vague, so I won't go into them now. Then the second girl disappeared."

"Yes."

"Well, if she was kidnapped, it means that the kidnappers didn't know about the murder, doesn't it? They didn't know she was the wrong girl."

"Unless, as we've thought, she may have been in on the kidnapping and hoped to get away with the ransom before the body of the real Holly was discovered."

"But what would have been the point of anyone taking all those risks and going to so much trouble when all they had to do was let Holly come here, then do a genuine kidnapping?"

I nodded. "Yes, I see. So the central question is why that other girl was planted on the Brightwells."

"And where she is now."

"Felix, you just said you'd some ideas about why she was sent here. Even if they're vague, tell me what they are."

He shook his head. "What I'm thinking about is what's happened to her. I believe she's in deadly danger. The victims of kidnapping always are. Once the ransom's been collected they're always liable to turn up dead, because they're probably able to identify the kidnappers."

"And I suppose the fact that they've blundered, as you said, makes things even worse for her, because actually she's useless to them and that's going to make them very angry. Only it's possible, isn't it, that they don't yet know they've blundered? If you're right that there've been two quite separate crimes, the kidnappers may not know about the murder, and if the girl has the sense to keep her mouth shut, they may go on hoping they can cash in on holding her."

I realized that Felix was not listening to me. His bright blue eyes, under their curiously drooping lids, had a glazed look as if they were looking at nothing and his thoughts had all turned inward.

"Blunders!" he suddenly exclaimed, but not as if he were speaking to me. He might have been talking to himself. "That's what's been at the back of my mind all along. That's why I've kept thinking about that stupid affair at school. I haven't thought about it for years and then it came back, wouldn't go away, I couldn't think why. I thought it was because of that man Ilsley reminding me of old Baldie—that's what we used to call our headmaster—but that's nonsense. The man's got nothing to do with it."

"Felix, would you mind telling me what you're talking about?" I said.

His eyes lost their glazed look as his attention snapped back to me. His journey into the unknown seemed to have done him good, for there was satisfaction in his tone as he said, "I think I'm beginning to get it sorted out. I'll explain presently. Now can I have another cup of tea?"

I poured out a second cup for each of us.

"But I still think we ought to tell the police about that knife having gone missing," I said. "The thought of it gives me a nasty sort of feeling. I'll do it if you don't want to."

"Perhaps you're right. All right, I'll do it." But he drank his tea before getting laboriously to his feet and starting towards the telephone.

As he lifted it, the front door bell rang.

He replaced the telephone.

"Are you expecting anyone?" he asked.

"No," I said.

"Then it's probably the police again. That'll save us a bit of trouble. We can tell them straightaway about the knife, including the fact that they'll find a beautiful set of my finger-prints on it. It may be good sense to tell them about that before they somehow find it out for themselves."

I went to the front door and opened it.

The two men who stood on the doorstep were not policemen. They were the two whom we had seen that morning in the Rose and Crown and for the first time in my life I found myself looking into the muzzle of a revolver.

# Chapter Eight

It was the small man who held it and it had a steely look of menace. What frightened me most about it, I think, was the feeling that the man was probably mad and so might do anything. No sane person could imagine he had any reason to point a gun at me. But one hears so often nowadays of women of eighty or more being murdered for the sake of the odd few pounds that they have in the house that it did not seem impossible that something horrible was about to happen.

"Where is she?" the small man said. "What have you done with her?"

I found the question reassuring in its way, because it seemed to indicate that he had not come to the house simply to murder me and steal my money.

"Who?" I asked.

"You know who I mean," he said. "Pam Pollett."

"I've never heard of anyone called Pam Pollett," I said.

"Oh yes, you have," he said. "And you know what's happened to her. We're coming in to look for her."

"Well, do, by all means," I said. "Look all over the house if you like. It'll surprise me very much if you find anyone."

I stood aside so that they could come in. At the same time Felix, who had recognized the voice of the small man, appeared in the doorway of the sitting room.

The man turned on him, waving the gun about in a way that I did not like.

"Come in and talk about what's on your mind, if you want to," Felix said, "but put that thing away. You don't need it against a woman and a man with a broken leg."

"Not till we've been through the house, we won't," the man said.

"That's right." The big man, who was standing a little behind his brother, made one of his rare contributions to the conversation.

"You go upstairs, Fred," the small man said. "I'll take the downstairs. And you two"—he waved the gun at Felix and me—"you go back into that room and stay there till we've had a look round. And don't try going near the telephone."

Obediently we went into the sitting room, followed by the small man, who looked round it carefully, including looking behind the curtains, which I had drawn when we came in, and behind the sofa, in case the person called Pam Pollett might be concealed there. Then he went out and by the sound of his footsteps I deduced that he had gone into the kitchen.

Overhead I heard the heavy tread of the big man, searching my bedroom.

"Pam Pollett," I said. "Is that the name of the girl who—"

Felix silenced me with a finger on his lips.

His face was alight with interest. He seemed to find nothing perturbing about our visitors, but rather something which he might almost have been hoping would happen. He nodded his head vigorously, but until the two men came into the room about a quarter of an hour later, he said nothing.

"Well, she's not here," the small man said. He was not holding the gun, so I supposed it was in a pocket or in a holster in his armpit, which is where detectives and gangsters usually keep them in television films. "Now are you going to tell us where she is, or do we have to go to work on you?" His strange, lashless eyes looked threatening.

"I think the best thing would be to have a drink," Felix said, "then talk the thing over in a civilized way. I assume this Pam you're talking about is the girl who's been staying with the Brightwells and who's disappeared. The funny thing is, I've been hoping you might be able to tell me something about her, but I didn't know how to get in touch with you. Not that I'm really involved, but I can't help wondering what's happened to her."

"There was nothing never said about kidnapping," the small man said, then broke off as Felix, who had crossed the room to the drinks tray, turned to look at him questioningly. He added, "Yes, whiskey. The same for my brother."

Felix poured out drinks for the four of us and brought them round. It was very unusual for him to drink whiskey, which he disliked and drank only in a more or less medicinal way. So he was either more agitated than he showed now and felt that it would steady him, or else felt that it would be tactful to drink the same as our visitors.

"Now let's sit down," he said, "and go into things quietly."

With some admiration, I realized that he was getting the upper hand of the two men. His behaviour was so unlike anything that they had expected that it bewildered them and then, once they had accepted his hospitality, or perhaps I should say mine, it put them at a disadvantage.

We all sat down.

He went on, "Kidnapping wasn't part of the plan, then?"

"You know it wasn't," the small man said.

Felix shook his head. "I've just had a feeling it wasn't. It's upset everything, hasn't it? You've had to stay around instead of getting the job done and getting away. I don't suppose you know what to do next. What does the boss say?"

"Here, you seem to know a lot about it," the small man said. "Are you in on it in some way?"

"No, but I know someone who is," Felix said. "Redman. Norman Redman. Isn't he the boss?"

The small man was silent, drinking some whiskey and frowning in intense concentration, trying to decide, I supposed, whether Felix really knew something or was just guessing.

I was asking myself the same question. For a moment after Felix had spoken, the name Redman had meant nothing to me, but then I remembered how he had told Inspector Roper that it had been a man called Redman with whom he had seen the girl we had all thought was Holly Noble in the Fox and Grapes. Felix had gone on to describe the man as a very bad character, and he had told the inspector how, when he had met the girl who was not Holly in Clyde Crendon's house, she had persuaded him to say nothing to the Brightwells about his previous brief meeting with her, on the grounds that she was trying very hard to make a new start in life.

"I don't say he is and I don't say he isn't," the small man said at last. "Redman's got a finger in a lot of things. The question is, where's the girl got to now? If we can't find her, we may as well give up and go home."

"Why not do that anyway?" Felix suggested.

"You seem to be mighty keen on it," the other said.

"I just don't like seeing people get into unnecessary trouble."

"It isn't because you're tied in with the police, like you were over the murder of that woman in Little Carberry Street? We heard about that."

"If I were, would I be advising you to get out? Wouldn't I be waiting to cop you when you did the job?"

"Well, maybe you would. But Redman's told us we've got to find Pam and I still got the feeling you could tell us where she is."

"Honest to God, I can't," Felix said.

The small man finished his drink. Standing up, he turned to his brother.

"Come on, drink up, we're only wasting our time here," he said. He looked again at Felix. "Maybe you don't know it and maybe you do and maybe we'll be back. If any harm's come to the girl, you'd better look out for yourself. Thanks for the drink, anyway. Come on, you."

He gave his brother a shove which made him get to his feet, though with a look of reluctance, as if he had hoped that they might be offered another drink before they left.

He followed his brother out of the room, neither Felix nor I thinking it necessary to show the two of them out of the house.

When we had heard the front door close behind them and a car drive away, I turned on Felix.

"What was all that about?" I demanded. "You do know something about what's happened."

"Oh yes, I know something now," he answered. "I know that Redman and those two men and the girl called Pam Pollett are all tied into something together, and I think I know a little more than that, but I'm not sure of it. There's the matter of a blunder which perhaps means something. On the other hand, it may have been just an accident. I think we'd better go and visit your friend, Clyde Crendon."

"Why d'you call him my friend?" I asked. "I don't know him any better than you do."

"Well, you've been avidly reading his books, which must have told you something about him that I don't know. Come on, let's go."

"What, now?"

I hated the thought of going out again that evening.

"The sooner the better," Felix said.

"I was just going to start cooking something for dinner."

"It can wait."

I had only been going to warm up some soup, grill some lamb chops and fry some frozen chips to go with them, so I could hardly complain that it could not possibly be delayed.

"But what do you want to see Clyde for?" I asked.

"It would be a bit complicated to explain," Felix said. "I've got to feel my way and see what I can get out of him."

"Well, before we go why don't you telephone the police and tell them about Hubert's knife being missing, as you were going to do before those men arrived?"

"I don't want to waste time. I think the sooner we get moving the better."

"But what's the connection with Clyde?"

"I hope to find out. Come on."

I let myself be hurried out by him.

It was dark outside and it felt even colder than before. Though it was not raining, there was a feeling of moisture in the air which made my face feel as if a damp, cold cloth were being pressed against it. I shivered and wondered why I had agreed to this visit to Clyde. Perhaps I already had some intuition of what Felix was going to say to him, but there was nothing clear in my mind, nothing on which I could have acted. And even if there had been, I doubt if I should have done anything about it. I should have stayed at home, grilled my lamb chops and left the responsibility of action to the police, who by now, for all I knew, had the whole problem sorted out.

I did not try to talk to Felix on the short drive to Clyde's house, the house with which he had fallen in love at first sight and which had seemed to me a homely, welcoming place on the one occasion when I had been in it. But now, in the light of the streetlamps, misted by the moisture in the air, it had a look of antique, chilling mystery. That could have been simply in my own mind, I knew, because I was apprehensive about what was going to happen, but still I felt it.

A light shone in only one window. I thought it was the window of the kitchen. All the rest of the house was in darkness. I parked the car at the gate and Felix and I walked up the path to the heavy oak door and Felix rattled on it with the doorknocker.

At first there was no reply and Felix was just going to knock again when a light was turned on in the hall inside and the door was opened by an elderly woman whom I recognized from my visit here for lunch as the housekeeper whom Ann had found for Clyde.

"Good evening," Felix said. "Can we see Mr. Crendon?"

"I'm not sure," the woman replied. "He isn't too well. I think he's lying down. But come in and I'll see how he is. Who shall I say it is?"

"Mr. and Mrs. Freer," Felix answered. "I don't like to disturb him if he isn't well, but it's a rather urgent matter. About a Miss Pollett, you might tell him."

She led the way to the sitting room that I remembered from our earlier visit and switched on the lights in it. The room was warm from the central heating and from the remains of a log fire that burned on the great open hearth. The woman stirred it up and added two or three logs to it.

"He didn't touch his lunch," she said. "That was before he went to see Lady Brightwell. And he's lying up there in the dark now, and he wouldn't have even a cup of tea when I went up to see how he was, and he won't let me call a doctor. I understand he was taken bad when he was over at Lady Brightwell's. So perhaps he won't be able to see you."

"I'm sorry," Felix said. "Is he often like this?"

"Never since I've known him, but that isn't very long. I think maybe it's a migraine, like my husband used to suffer with. Knocked him out for a whole day sometimes and there was nothing he could do about it but take the pills they gave him and they never did much good. He used just to have to wait till the trouble passed off at last. If that's what's wrong with Mr. Crendon I don't suppose he'll come down now."

"I understand," Felix said. "We'll wait."

She left us and I heard her climbing the stairs.

"Do you mean you want to wait here till his migraine goes off?" I said. "That might be hours."

"It isn't a migraine he's suffering from," Felix said. "It's simply terror at having got in out of his depth. And I think he'll see us if the Pollett girl is mentioned."

"You aren't suggesting he kidnapped her, are you?"

"We'll see."

The new logs on the fire were crackling and flames were leaping up the chimney. I moved closer to it and held out my hands to it.

"You're enjoying yourself," I said. "You know, Felix, you ought to have joined the police when you were young. You like hunting people down. I've seen you at it before."

He shook his head. "I'm not hunting anyone down. In a way, I'm doing the opposite. I'm here to deliver a warning."

❀ ❀ ❀

There was a sound at the door and we both turned.

Clyde was standing there, wearing his shabby trousers and heavy pullover, and with his thin, straw-coloured hair standing up spikily on his head. The lids of his grey eyes were red and swollen. I wondered if that could be a symptom of a migraine, or meant simply that he had been crying. His face was as pale as when I had seen him last.

"I'm sorry to have kept you waiting," he said. "Sit down. You'll have a drink, won't you? What will you have? Whiskey? Gin?"

"Nothing for me, thank you," Felix said.

I did not want anything either, though I thought that I should probably want a drink very badly when we got home.

"Well, you won't mind if I go ahead and have one," Clyde said. "I haven't been feeling too good since I made that exhibition of myself at the Brightwells'." He turned to a tray of drinks on a side table and poured out a large whiskey for himself. Felix and I both sat down, but Clyde remained standing in front of the fire. "I understand there's something urgent you wanted to say to me."

"About Pam Pollett," Felix said.

A muscle in Clyde's cheek began to twitch, but he said, "Who's she?"

"The girl who's been staying at the Brightwells' and who's gone."

"Is that her name? Pam Pollett." Clyde seemed to repeat the name to himself and to give it some thought. "How did you find it out?"

"From Norman Redman's two friends, the men with whom we had a chat this morning in the Rose and Crown," Felix answered.

"Is that who they were? Not that I know who Norman Redman is. But it was a curious sort of scene they made, wasn't it?"

"Not so very curious when you realize they were simply doing their best to warn you against me."

"But why should they think of doing that?"

"Clyde, I believe it would save us a lot of trouble if you were to let me go ahead and tell you what I know and how I got to know it and then ask you some questions afterwards."

"But I don't understand..." Clyde began on a note of protest. His voice was thick, as if he had a cold, or, as I had thought on first seeing him, he had been crying. He shrugged his shoulders and took a gulp of whiskey. "All right, go ahead. What's on your mind?"

"The murder of Holly Noble, but some other things before that. It began, I think, the first time you saw the Baraud painting in the Brightwells' house. *Le Rapas en plein air*. It bowled you over, didn't it? I believe you're given to falling in love at first sight, as you did with this house. If Ann had been willing to part with the picture, you'd have written her a cheque on the spot. But she'd no intention of parting with it, so you hatched a scheme of how you could get hold of it. Or did somebody else hatch it for you? I think that's more likely. Was it Pam Pollett, or did you go direct to Redman?"

Clyde, having allowed Felix to go ahead, only closed his soft, full lips into an unusually firm line and did not answer.

"My guess is, though you can correct me if I'm wrong," Felix went on, "that you knew Pam quite well and confided in her your longing to get hold of the picture, and she put you in touch with Redman. I'd seen them together in a pub called the Fox and Grapes, so I knew she knew him. I'd chatted with the two of them there for a bit, though it happened that nobody mentioned her name to me on that occasion. So when I met her down here and recognized her, it didn't occur to me that she wasn't Holly Noble. It did strike me as odd that she should have been in the Fox and Grapes when she was said to have been studying music in Rome, but I supposed she'd either been on vacation, or perhaps had been sneaking a visit back to London for reasons of her own. Then when she and I talked here at your lunch party, she asked me particularly not to mention that I'd seen her with Redman and his crowd, because she'd got involved with them when she was practically a kid and she was trying to break away from them, but she was scared of what they might do to her because she knew so much about them, and this chance of living with the Brightwells was a wonderful opportunity for her. Like a mug, I almost believed her."

Clyde had finished his drink and had sat down and was gently rocking backwards and forwards with his hands pressed together between his knees. I thought for a moment that he was going to speak, but then he only gave a slight shudder and glared down with a look of fierce concentration at his hands.

"I think I know what you nearly said then," Felix said. "Why didn't I *quite* believe her? Why had I any doubts? Because I did have them even then. I didn't know why myself at the time. It was just a feeling that I'd seen something or heard something that didn't fit in with what she'd told me. But it didn't seem important to me then and I wished her luck if she was trying to carve out a better life for herself. I only began to worry when I saw those two characters we saw this morning in the Rose and Crown and it was obvious that they were down here to do a job. I'd often seen the small chap in the Fox and Grapes with Redman's crowd and I recognized him at once. He recognized me too and the two of them cleared out as quickly as they could. But because I knew that Holly, or Pam, or whatever you want to call her, had been in with that lot, I started to ask myself if the job that couple were here to do could have anything to do with the Baraud paintings. And if it had, then Holly's job down here was simply to let them into the house. The first thing Hubert did when he and Ann discovered the value of the paintings was to have new and very sophisticated locks fitted on all the doors and windows, so someone had to be got inside the house who could make sure that a door would be left open. She couldn't pull off the theft alone because those pictures, particularly the one in the hall that you like so much, are pretty large and heavy. Two men at least were needed. And also an empty house was needed so that they could go ahead with taking the pictures down and loading them into a van that they'd have had waiting outside without being interrupted. But there they ran into a difficulty they hadn't expected. The Santos couple hardly ever go out, and if they did go out one day and Hubert and Ann happened to go out at the same time, I was likely to be in the house, working. So instead of being able to get the job done in a few days and Pam being able to disappear, there was delay, and before they could decide what to do about it, she was kidnapped."

Clyde's rocking backwards and forwards had stopped and he had released his hands.

"This is all very interesting," he said, "and, for all I know, may be perfectly correct. It sounds very plausible. But where do I come in?"

"The maddening thing about that," Felix said, "is that I had the clue to the girl's connection with you almost from the start and I didn't give it a thought till today when I suddenly remembered something that happened to me at school. I told Virginia about it this morning and even then the penny didn't drop. I was good at maths, you see, and I had a nice little racket going of doing my homework and then flogging my results to my friends at a bob a time. And then one day I was careless and I made two mistakes in my work, and so all the others had exactly the same two mistakes in theirs and I was caught. And that's what you and Pam did. You made the same mistake. And I didn't think it was in the least important."

Clyde's eyes were on Felix now, the eyes that seemed so inappropriately alert and observant in his plump, almost child-like face.

"Well?" he said after a moment. Then as Felix remained silent, he went on, "Like most other people, I've made a great many mistakes in my life and it would be astonishing if one or two of them didn't coincide with some which, say, Virginia had made, or this girl Pam, or even you."

"That's true," Felix agreed. "And if there weren't a few other things to back up my theory, I'd drop it as merely fantastic. When those two men made that scene this morning that I couldn't understand, and it sounded to me as if they could be warning you that I couldn't be trusted because once or twice in my time I've helped the police with a murder, I thought the idea was too fantastic to be taken seriously. But it stayed at the back of my mind, and then this thing about two people making the same mistake suddenly struck me and how it could have been you who got Pam into the Brightwells' house after the real Holly had been murdered."

"Murder, murder!" Clyde cried out suddenly, his voice rising to a falsetto shriek. He pounded his knees with his fists. "Why are you trying to tie me in with the murder? Is it because of the way I fainted at the Brightwells' when the rest of you were talking about that girl having her throat cut? D'you think it was because I was frightened? Let me tell you, the first thing I knew about the murder was when you told me about it outside the supermarket. It nearly made me ill then. And the first thing I knew about its being the real Holly who was murdered was when I heard it from Virginia, when she was telling Ann about it. And I don't know why I fainted except that at that point I just passed out. I've been horribly squeamish all my life. If I see real dead bodies—not just actors pretending to be dead—you can always tell the difference—I shut my eyes. I sometimes think that's why I write the sort of books I do. I'm trying to get over my wretched weakness."

Felix nodded. There was some sympathy in his expression.

"Yes, that's how I thought it was," he said. "I was pretty sure that the trouble was that you couldn't bear your own responsibility for the girl's murder, even though you never intended it to happen. I know you didn't intend it."

"Responsibility?" Clyde squeaked in the same odd, high voice. "I'm not responsible for anything."

"But at least you've just admitted you knew there was a real and an unreal Holly," Felix said, sounding sorry for Clyde for having made such a clumsy mistake. It was not the sort of thing that he would ever have done himself. "And you were upset enough at the supermarket, as you said, when I told you about the murder and you thought it was Pam. All the same, it didn't hit you too hard then because even if it distressed you, you knew you had nothing to do with it. It was when you heard it was the real Holly who'd been killed, and you realized that you were responsible, even though it had never occurred to you that her murder was almost inevitable, that you blacked out. But now let's get on to Lady Macbeth."

Clyde stared at Felix as if he could not believe that he had heard him correctly.

"In God's name, what's *she* got to do with it?"

"That mistake you made," Felix answered. "That you and Pam both made. That blunder. You both said it was Roger Cairns in *Macbeth* with Sara Noble, when really it was James Calvin."

"Was it?" Clyde asked vaguely. "That's the sort of mistake I often make. I'm not good at names. It doesn't mean anything. I don't see why you should think it does."

"Only because Pam made the same mistake, and she was supposed to be Sara Noble's daughter. It didn't seem a likely mistake for her to have made, unless someone had coached her in it mistakenly, specially as she seemed to know a fair amount about her mother's life in the theatre, but nothing else about her. I gather she never said anything personal about her, or about her own background either. She was careful to keep that down to a minimum, as I expect you'd told her she should."

"I see," Clyde said and gave a deep sigh. He gave a little shrug of defeat. "Yes, it was careless of me. I should have done my homework better, as you should have done yours with your maths. I'll admit I'd concocted a scheme to get hold of the Barauds. But d'you know, I never really took it seriously?

You may not believe it, but I thought of it almost as a joke. Getting mixed up in a real crime, I mean, instead of just writing about it. Somehow, right up to the time Pam turned up here, I didn't feel it was actually going to happen. Once she did arrive I got scared and wanted to call the whole thing off, but that day when you all came to lunch with me she told me pretty firmly that she and Redman had already gone to a lot of trouble getting her into the house, and that if I didn't want to stay mixed up in the plot, they'd go ahead with it on their own. The Baraud pictures could be worth a lot, she said, even if I didn't want them, and if I thought of putting a stop to the plan she'd tell the Brightwells just how deep in I'd been. So I did nothing. I just hoped that somehow it wouldn't come off and nothing would happen. And I swear I didn't know they'd got Pam into the house by murdering Holly and sending Pam in her place."

"What did you plan to do with the paintings, once you'd got them?" Felix asked curiously. "You could hardly have hung them up here."

"I hadn't really thought that out," Clyde said. "I've got a house in Tuscany and I think I'd have shipped them out there."

"How did you meet Pam?"

"Oh, at some party. I remember I said to her more or less flippantly at that first meeting that I wondered what it felt like to commit a real crime, and she said I ought to meet a friend of hers, and the friend was Redman. I met the two of them several times after that, and once, after one or two drinks too many, I told them the only things I'd ever wanted to steal were some pictures in the house of some friends of mine. And so somehow the plan grew." He paused and thrust his hands between his knees again and resumed his rocking backwards and forwards. "No, I'm not speaking the truth. I got scared all right, but I wanted to go ahead with the scheme. But not with murder. I swear I didn't know anything about the murder." His voice began to go falsetto again. "So the funny thing is, I haven't committed any crime at all. I conspired to commit a crime, but the crime hasn't happened. The pictures haven't been stolen. So that doesn't count, does it? And I didn't know anything about the murder."

"But murder was inevitable, wasn't it?" Felix said.

"You said that before," Clyde said in that unnaturally high voice. "I don't see why."

'Because Holly could identify whoever it was who got her out of the way. Who was it? Redman?"

"I don't know. I don't know how they did it."

"Do you know how they made contact with her in Rome? I suppose they'd have heard through you that Ann was going to meet her at Heathrow. You got that out of Ann, didn't you, and the number of the plane she was arriving on?"

"Yes." Clyde gave another deep sigh and let his voice drop down to a husky whisper. "Yes, I did that."

"And her address in Rome?"

"The address of the academy where she was studying."

"So Redman must have got in touch with her by telephone there and said he was Hubert and that she was to come on an earlier plane and that it was he who'd meet her and bring her home. And she was to wear the white flower she'd agreed on with Ann so that he could pick her up. And as she'd never met Hubert she didn't know the man who met her was someone else and she went with him quite confidently, and he drove off into Sussex, killed her, and dumped her body in a pond. D'you know, when I first started to work this out, I thought it could actually have been Hubert who carried it all out, but Virginia persuaded me that was nonsense. But I still believed I'd hit on the method that was used. Pam, I assumed, had flown off to Rome and came back on the right plane to be met by Ann. And it all went wonderfully smoothly. But they had to kill Holly, you see, because if they'd let her go she'd always have been able to identify Redman."

"I wish I was dead," Clyde said abruptly.

"Oh come, that's going a bit far," Felix said. "As you said, by chance you haven't actually committed a crime. Whoever kidnapped Pam prevented that. But I'm curious what you mean to do about the whole thing."

"Hang myself," Clyde answered.

"No, you mustn't do that," Felix protested. "It's so unfair on the people who find you and have to cut you down. They may be just as squeamish as you are. I suppose you don't know, incidentally, who's kidnapped Pam."

"Of course not."

"Are you sure? Would you let me, for instance, take a quick look through this house?"

"Look anywhere you bloody well please."

Felix seemed to think about it, then stood up. "I don't think I'll trouble. It really doesn't make sense for you to have kidnapped her. You knew all along she wasn't the right girl. Virginia, let's go."

Clyde jumped to his feet.

"What are you going to do?"

"Go home," Felix said.

"Aren't you going to the police?"

"What for?"

"To tell them all this."

"I'd far sooner you did it yourself. Have you considered doing that? I don't consort with the police any more than I have to. But it might not be a bad idea for you to help them with their inquiries, though perhaps that depends on what's happened to Pam. Anyway, Virginia and I will leave you in peace now."

He moved towards the door.

I started to follow him, then I stopped.

"Clyde, you aren't really going to do anything foolish, are you?"

"What could be more foolish than what I've already done?" he asked. "You don't know how I've been feeling since I heard of that girl's death. I don't suppose I shall ever get it out of my mind. It'll always be there, guilt for the death of someone innocent and trusting. I won't be able to live with it."

"If you talk like that Felix and I will phone the police and stay here till they come," I said.

Felix took me by the arm. "Come along," he said. "Let the man make his own mind up."

"Yes, go—for God's sake, go!" Clyde muttered at us, then suddenly shrieked, "Go on, get out!"

I let Felix pull me out to the front door, then through it into the darkness.

But at the gate I stood still again. The headlights of a car cruising past were foggy in the moisture-laden air and lit up an expression of greater strain than I had expected on Felix's face.

"Felix, suppose he does hang himself, or take an overdose of pills or something. I think we ought to go back," I said.

"He won't do anything like that," Felix replied.

"Do you mean you really think he'll go to the police and confess?"

"Oh no, I shouldn't think he'll do that either."

"Then what's he going to do? If he does kill himself, it'll be almost as if we'd murdered him."

"I don't think there's much risk of it. Just as he kidded himself that the crime he was going to commit was all a joke, he's only kidding himself now when he says he can't live with what he's done. My guess is he'll be off within an hour or so to that house of his in Tuscany. I shouldn't be surprised if he's on the telephone already, finding out when the next plane leaves for those parts. Then he'll probably settle down there peacefully and write another thriller."

"What about extradition?"

"I believe it's slow and complicated. And the police may pick up Redman, if he's the man who actually murdered Holly. Then they won't be very interested in Clyde. Do come along. I'm hungry. I want something to eat."

"You aren't going to tell the police what you worked out about the plot to steal the Barauds?"

"Why should I? They haven't been stolen."

"D'you know, I think you wanted to talk to Clyde only to warn him that he ought to get out of the way in a hurry?" I said. "It doesn't seem to worry you that even if he didn't actually commit the crime, he meant to."

"Well, I can't help feeling sorry for him. Poor old Clyde is just an amateur when it comes to crime."

"It's funny, that's just what he said about you and your ghostwriting."

"And that was true, wasn't it?"

We got into the car and started for home.

It had been an exhausting day and I felt too tired to do any cooking that evening, even to grill the chops that I had bought, so I made some sandwiches and we ate them sitting by the fire.

I could not stop thinking about Clyde. Felix had sounded very sure of himself when he said that there was no risk that he would commit suicide and for the time being he had convinced me of it. But I had always had a tendency to let him convince me of the most improbable things, and even now, when I knew only too well how little he was to be relied on, I found it difficult to fight my own inclination to believe him. I began to think that without consulting him I would go out, drive back to Clyde's house, and find out how things were with him. I was not going to feel easy in my mind till I had done that.

I was just about to get to my feet to leave the house quietly and return to my car when the telephone rang.

I started and wanted to shout at it to stop. Every time that it had rung during the last few days it had meant trouble of some kind. I felt a hysterical hatred of it and tried willing myself to sit still and ignore it. But it was useless. I can never leave a telephone unanswered and though Felix made no move to go to it and did not even suggest that it might be a good thing if I did, when it had rung ten times I gave in and picked it up.

It was Ann.

"Virginia, an extraordinary thing has happened," she said. "I thought I ought to tell you about it straightaway. It may help to set your mind at rest. They've got the man who murdered Holly."

My mind was so much on Clyde that all that I could think of for the moment was that he had been arrested.

"Oh?" I said in a stupid sort of voice.

"I don't mean they've charged him yet, or that they've allowed his name to be quoted," she went on. "He's only helping them with their inquiries. But they've told us about it and how they got him. It's a man called Redman. I understand it's partly thanks to something Felix told them that they've got him. Felix told them he'd seen the man with Pam Pollett—that's the real name of the girl who's been staying with us—in some London pub. And they'd got pictures of him because he's been in trouble with them before, and they tried them out on various people who travelled from Rome in the same plane with Holly. It was an earlier plane than the one I met. And two or three of them have identified him as a man they saw meet Holly when she got to Heathrow. He's a fairly conspicuous man with a long white face and quite bald. I don't quite understand his motive, but it's something to do with a plot to steal our Barauds. It's all very extraordinary, but the police seem quite sure they've got the right man." She paused, and after a moment, as I had said nothing, she added, "You don't seem very interested."

"Oh, I am—very interested," I said, trying to sound as if I were, when really a dreadful weariness had suddenly descended on me, a kind of blankness which nearly blotted out the meaning of what she had said. What was it, after all, but confirmation of Felix's theory about the crime? "I'm glad they've got him. But have you had any instructions yet from the kidnappers about what to do with the ransom for Pam?"

"No."

"Nothing at all?"

"Nothing."

Behind me I heard Felix mutter something to attract my attention.

"Hold on a moment, Ann," I said. "I think Felix wants to tell me something to say to you." I cupped my hand over the telephone and looked round at him. "What is it?"

"Tell her there aren't going to be any instructions," he said, "because the kidnappers already know the real Holly is dead."

"How d'you know?"

"Never mind. Just tell her that."

I spoke into the telephone again, repeating Felix's message.

"I don't know how he knows it," I said, "or what he means by it, but anyway, that's what he says."

"Does he mean—?" She stopped, and I heard her sharp little intake of breath. "No, how could he know a thing like that? Well, good night, Virginia. I only rang because I thought you'd like to know what's been happening."

"Yes, thank you, Ann. Good night."

We both rang off.

I turned to Felix and I was going to ask him why he was so sure that there would be no instructions about the ransom for Pam when I realized that a noise in the garden that had been going on all the time I had been speaking to Ann had suddenly grown louder. It was the barking of a dog, a dog which I knew belonged to my neighbours and which was usually allowed out into their garden at about this time in the evening.

It very seldom barked, except occasionally at someone passing, and its behaviour this evening was quite exceptional, for it was not only keeping up a continuous yelping, but there was a sound of frenzy in it which turned into an eerie howling. I wondered if it could have been hurt. It was very traffic-conscious and seldom strayed out into the road, but it might have done so for once and been hit by a car.

"There's something wrong with that dog," I said. "I'm going out to see what it is."

I went out into the garden, leaving the front door open behind me.

Light from the door fell along the path to the gate and there was a streetlamp too just outside it and I saw that the dog had come into my garden. It was a big, cream-coloured Labrador, usually the friendliest, most tranquil of animals, but now it was standing on the path, its legs rigid, its head tilted up, baying hysterically. At the same time I saw something else on the path.

It was a shoe. And close to it the foot that it had belonged to, from which it must have fallen off, projected a little way from behind a lilac bush that grew beside the gate. When I went towards it, I saw the rest of the body lying between the bush and the low brick wall that edged my garden.

It was Pam Pollett and she was lying face downwards on the damp earth. In the misty light from the streetlamp I saw the haft of the knife that had been driven into her back.

# Chapter Nine

The police arrived only a few minutes after I had dialled 999.

By then Felix had taken over. He had managed to persuade the dog to go back to the house where he belonged and had remained waiting at the gate for the police car, while I had sat down in the sitting room, shivering with shock. The front door had been left open and the cold air that seeped in through it seemed to come straight to me from that dreadfully cold body in the garden.

For some time none of the police came into the house. I could hear their voices outside and I heard more than one car arrive, and once or twice while I sat there I felt that I ought to go out and see what was happening. But what was the point of doing that? When they wanted me they could come in and find me.

In the meantime I only wanted to get as close to the fire as I could. I added coal to it, poked it up into a blaze and crouched over it.

I have no idea how long it was before Felix came in. It felt an unbearably long time, but perhaps it was only about twenty minutes. Like me, he seemed to need to get close to the fire.

Standing on the hearthrug, he put an elbow on the mantelpiece, leant his head on his hand, and gazed down into the flames.

For a moment he did not speak, then he said in a low voice, as if he were afraid that the men in the garden might overhear him, "I've been such a fool. I thought I knew everything. But I never thought a thing like this could happen."

"What was it you thought you knew?" I asked.

"Oh, who the kidnappers were," he answered. "I've been sure of it ever since we talked to Clyde and realized he couldn't have had anything to do with it. But I didn't really think they'd take to murder. Not that it wasn't too late already by the time we'd seen him. The police think she was killed sometime in the afternoon."

"Who do you think they were?" I inquired.

"Tim and Barbie," he said shortly.

I had a puzzled sort of feeling that I had not heard him correctly.

"When did you think of that?"

"Well, in a way, right at the beginning when Pam disappeared and we still thought she was Holly. They had a motive, you see."

I shook my head. "No, I don't see."

"They were expecting to inherit the Brightwells' money, weren't they? And Hubert and Ann have often helped them out already. For instance, they bought the Hallidays' cottage for them. But if Ann was going to fall in love with that girl who they thought was Holly Noble and start to lavish her wealth on her, their pickings might not have been so good. But as it happened, I was quite wrong about that. It had very little to do with why they kidnapped her, though perhaps it has something to do with her murder."

"Why did they kidnap her?"

"Simply for the ransom. I've heard *The Platform* is in a pretty rocky state. I think both of them are expecting to be out of a job fairly soon, so I suppose they need money. And they knew Ann, you see. They thought she'd want to pay even though she'd known the girl for such a short time."

"But they meant to murder her from the beginning?"

"It seems likely. If they'd let her go she'd always have been a danger to them. What I'm not sure of is why they killed her when they discovered she wasn't Holly. She was worthless to them for ransom purposes from the time the real Holly was found. She was just a petty crook whose plan had come unstuck. They could quite safely have let her go. She wouldn't have risked making a fuss about it. But what I think happened then, though I'm only guessing, is that she tried to blackmail them, threatening to tell the Brightwells how they'd abducted her, and that could have ruined their prospects with the Brightwells, even if she wasn't the right girl."

"You're sure of what you're saying, Felix?" I said. "You aren't just making all this up to impress the police?"

"I'm quite sure of it."

"Oh dear, Tim and Barbie have always seemed to me such nice people." I moved an inch or two closer to the fire. "For one thing, they're so happily married and that's always nice to see."

"Didn't we agree the Macbeths were a very happily married couple?"

"How much of this have you told the police?" I asked.

"Only where to look for traces of where she's been kept," he said. "There hasn't been time for anything else."

"And what are they doing about it?"

"I don't know. But it didn't really seem to come as a surprise to them just now." He sounded resentful, as if his own intelligence had been exploited. "They'd worked it out for themselves it was an inside job. In the first place, there was the question of how she'd been picked up quietly in the middle of Allingford. The most probable thing was that it was by someone she knew, and she didn't know many people here. Then later there was the information they'd had from Hubert about the knife from his study being missing, and when they saw it stick out of Pam's back they asked me if that was the knife and I said it looked like it. So then they asked me who'd been in the house when it vanished and I told them that besides the Brightwells there'd been you and me and Clyde and Barbie and Tim. And I told them that they should expect to find my fingerprints on it, but that didn't seem to interest them. Actually I don't suppose they're there anymore, because Tim and Barbie will have been careful to polish the haft in case any of their own were on it. Anyway, before I'd finished, that man Roper sent a couple of men off in a car, and whether they were going to Clyde's house or to Tim and Barbie's cottage, I don't know."

"Roper's out there now, is he?" I asked.

"Yes."

"He'll be coming in here presently, I suppose."

"I expect so."

"Then before he does, I want a drink. What about you?"

Felix moved away from the fireplace and flung himself down on the sofa.

"Yes, all right. But why do I always seem to drink so much when I'm with you? When I'm alone I hardly drink at all. Do you drink more or less when you're alone?"

"Less, I think." I got up and poured out whiskey for each of us. "Somehow we only seem to meet when there's a crisis of some sort, and then of course it helps."

"I suppose it's a crisis for you, just having me to stay with you. But I hope you don't turn into one of those old women who keep on tippling away all day and are never really sober. Then one day they trip up and fall down the stairs and break their necks."

"I dare say there are worse deaths. At least I expect it's over quickly. Felix—"

"Yes?"

"What did you tell the police about Clyde?"

"Nothing except that he was in the Brightwells' house when the knife disappeared."

"Why not?"

"The fact is, I rather like the little man. And he's got so hopelessly out of his depth. It made me want to help him. I hope he gets safely away to his house in Tuscany. For one thing, you like his books and I shouldn't like the supply of them to stop."

"But he was trying to pull off a major burglary," I reminded him.

"But he didn't succeed. I've always a certain sympathy for people who are hopeless failures."

"One can hardly call him a failure—not with his income."

"As a criminal he was. And I'm sure he'll never try anything of the sort again. He'll stick to the job he can do."

"Well, as a matter of fact, I'm glad you didn't say anything about him." The whiskey inside me was warming me better than the fire. "There's something about him that makes one feel protective. Now let me get it straight how you worked it out that Tim and Barbie were the kidnappers. It began, you said, with the question of how she was picked up in the middle of Allingford."

"Yes, and there were three possible explanations of that. One was that she'd been picked up by a stranger and been murdered and dumped somewhere. One was that she'd been picked up by arrangement and was faking her own kidnapping. And one was that she'd been picked up by someone she knew and taken away and genuinely kidnapped. I gave up the first idea when I heard about the death of the real Holly and realized the girl here was an impostor with a difficult game to play, who wouldn't have risked going anywhere with a stranger in case it upset the more important plan. I gave up the second idea when I found out from Clyde what the game was. There was no room in it for a kidnapping. So that left the third possibility. She'd been given a lift by someone she knew and hidden probably somewhere close. But there was something that puzzled me about that. Why had it been done when she'd been with the Brightwells such a very short time? And the answer to that seemed to be that it was done by someone who knew she didn't mean to stay around for long. Someone who'd had a chance to see that she was restless and bored and anxious to get away. If the job was to pulled off at all, it had to be soon. And so far as I knew, the only people who'd had a chance to observe that, apart from us and the Brightwells, were the Hallidays and Clyde. And when I crossed Clyde off the list after our visit to him this evening, that left Tim and Barbie. That's all, really. It's for the police to tie up all the loose ends."

"But why did they dump the body in our garden, of all places?" I asked.

"I've got a theory about that," Felix answered. "I think they wanted to dump it on someone who'd had a chance to get at the knife, and that meant Clyde or us. And their first idea was Clyde. Do you remember, when we were leaving his house and were standing at his gate, a car went by?"

"Vaguely," I said.

"Well, I think Tim and Barbie were in that car with the body. And if we hadn't been at the gate, they'd have taken it into Clyde's garden and hidden it somewhere there."

"But they didn't even try to hide it in ours," I said. "They left it right by the gate, where it was bound to be found soon."

"Because of the dog. If he hadn't come rushing out and raised the alarm, I think they'd have carried the body round to the back of the house and put it in your coal cellar, or somewhere like that. But as it was, they just shoved it in behind the lilac bush and made off as fast as they could."

"And went back to the cottage?"

"More likely to London, I should think. Tracking them down is a job for the police, as well as finding proof that they'd anything whatever to do with the kidnapping and the murder. I've done all I can for them."

"Well, I hope we hear how that goes sooner or later."

We did, but not that evening. After a time Inspector Roper came in and asked me to recount how I had found Pam Pollett's body when I went out because the dog was barking. I had been reared in the belief that policemen did not drink when they were on duty, but he did not refuse a whiskey. Presently the voices in the garden faded. What I thought sounded like an ambulance came and went away. Inspector Roper announced that it had been a long day and that he was very tired. For the first time I felt that he was human. Then he went away. I shut the front door behind him and returned to the fireside.

All of a sudden a strange stillness seemed to fall upon the house. I wished that I was already in bed and could simply go to sleep, but to go upstairs seemed almost too much of an effort to contemplate. With some dismay, I remembered that tomorrow was Monday and that I had a full morning of appointments at the clinic ahead of me. I should have liked it to be a very quiet day which I had all to myself without murder, without policemen, without the Brightwells. And, yes, without Felix...

❁ ❁ ❁

I was not sure if he had fallen asleep on the sofa, but he was lying quite still with his eyes closed, so after a little while I forced myself to get up and go to bed. In spite of my tiredness I did not expect to sleep much, but almost at once I fell into a deep and healing slumber.

I got through my busy morning next day with some difficulty, had lunch in the canteen at the clinic, then, instead of returning home, went to the Brightwells. I ought to look in on Ann, I thought, and see how she was. I supposed the police would have told her and Hubert by now about Pam Pollett's murder, though I did not know whether or not they would have mentioned that Tim and Barbie were suspects. So far as I knew both the Brightwells were fond of them and if they had been told that their nephew and niece were wanted by the police for murder, it would have been a very heavy blow for them to bear. If they had not already been told this, I had no intention of saying anything about it.

But as soon as I saw them I knew that they had been told the whole story. Both their faces were pale and tired, as if they had had no sleep, and when Santos ushered me into the drawing room, Ann said swiftly, "Don't talk about it. It's all over now. They've arrested Tim and Barbie, you know, and I believe Felix had something to do with it, but I don't want to talk about it. Let me tell you about the Barauds. We've decided to sell them. After what's happened I could never look at them without remembering it all, and somehow we've got to put it behind us. A man's coming down from Christie's tomorrow to look at the pictures."

"I believe selling them is what Ann really wants to do now," Hubert said in an apologetic tone, wanting to make it clear that he had put no pressure on her to do so. There was something unfamiliarly gentle in their attitudes to one another. "If we get a good price for them we could start shopping around to see if we can find something to put in their place. In any case, we've decided to take a trip abroad. We'll go round the world, I think. Go by sea and take a nice long time about it. And on the way I might get down to writing that autobiography of mine. I believe a long sea voyage, with no distractions, is a splendid time for writing. Which reminds me, I owe Felix some money. Just wait a moment, I'll write him a cheque."

"Don't bother about that now," I said.

"Best to do it right away."

He went out of the room, I supposed to his study, to get the cheque written.

"What's happened to Mr. Ilsley?" I asked Ann. "Has he gone home?"

"Yes, I believed he stayed the night in Allingford, but he left this morning," she replied. "He telephoned before he left. And Clyde Crendon's gone away too. Did you know that?"

"No," I said.

"I suppose he found life in Allingford too hectic," she said with a wry little smile. "I believe he's got a house somewhere in Italy and he's going there. It was funny, he rang up yesterday evening to say goodbye and to thank me for having been so good to him. All I did for him was find him a housekeeper, but he said he would always remember me. It sounded as if he wasn't coming back."

So Norman Redman had not talked yet and Clyde had got away without being suspected of any connection with the attempted theft of the Barauds. But I could not help wondering if, when the pictures were put up for sale at Christie's, someone there might not put in a bid for an anonymous client in Tuscany.

Hubert came back into the room with a cheque made out to Felix. Considering how little work he had done and how unqualified he had been to do that little, the amount was generous.

Presently, when I gave it to Felix, he gave a nod of satisfaction and said, "That solves one thing, anyway."

"What's that?" I asked.

"How I'm to get back to London. I don't think I could cope with a train yet, and I couldn't really expect you to drive me up. But now I can afford a hired car. I expect you know of some taxi people here who do that sort of thing."

Since a number of my patients who come to the clinic and who are too lame to walk arrive by taxi or hired car, I was able to give him the telephone number of a firm that would send a car to take him to London, but before ringing them up he set about packing his small suitcase.

While he was doing it, I said, "Of course you'll have to come back for the inquest."

"Yes, but with luck I'll have got rid of this by then—" He knocked the plaster on his leg with a knuckle. "So I'll be more mobile and I'll probably just come down for the day. I don't suppose it'll happen in any great hurry. The forensic people will probably want to go over Tim and Barbie's cottage and over the Pollett girl's clothes to see if there's any real evidence they kept her there. And there's the car too in which they brought her here. However careful they were, there may be bloodstains in it. It's extraordinary what those people can find out nowadays."

He turned out to be right, though I did not hear this for some days. There were some traces of blood that matched Pam's in the car and there was some dust with carpet fibres in it on her clothes that matched the carpet in an attic in the cottage. And Tim and Barbie were arrested and were later found guilty. And Hubert and Ann went away on their world cruise, though I do not believe that Hubert's autobiography ever got written. But that was all in the future as I watched Felix close his suitcase and reach for the telephone. A car, he was told, would pick him up in a quarter of an hour.

While we sat waiting for it, I said, "I hope Hermione will look after you properly."

"I'm sure she will," he said. "As I told you, she's a dear girl."

There had been a number of dear girls in his life and I had always felt an irrational jealousy of them, which I hoped he did not perceive, as there was certainly no justification for me to feel it. It was my own fault that I would never again be one of them.

The soft toot of a horn in the road told us when the car arrived. Felix stood up, put an arm round me, and kissed me on the cheek.

"How does that rhyme go?" he said. " 'I met Murder in the way—He had the mask of Halliday...' No, no," he went on quickly as I was about to protest at the misquotation, "I wasn't going to say it was thinking of that rhyme that put me onto Tim and Barbie. It was rather the other way round. The name Halliday at the back of my mind made me dredge up that rhyme from God knows where. Goodbye for now, darling Virginia. And I hope we don't meet any more murders for the present, though if I should come across that little bastard on a bicycle who knocked me down, I should take the greatest pleasure in strangling him. It would be a case of justifiable homicide."

We hope you liked *I Met Murder* and that you'll permit us a recommendation for more in the mould of the classic British whodunit. The Henry Tibbett series, by Patricia Moyes, is traditional but never stodgy, and, like the Ferrars books, full of sharp detail. We've included an excerpt from the first installment, *Dead Men Don't Ski*. Enjoy!

# Dead Men Don't Ski

## Chapter One

It was just nine o'clock on a cold and clammy January morning when Chief Inspector Henry Tibbett's taxi drew up outside the uninviting cavern of Victoria Station. From the suburban lines the Saturday morning hordes of office-bound workers streamed anxiously through the barriers to bus and underground—pale, strained faces, perpetually in a hurry, perpetually late: but here, at this side-entrance that led into a sort of warehouse fitted with an imposing array of weighing-platforms, were assembled a group of people who looked as paradoxical at that hour and place as a troupe of Nautch girls at the Athenæum. They were not all young, Henry noted with relief, though the average age was certainly under thirty: but young or middle-aged, male or female, all were unanimous in their defiant sartorial abandon— the tightest trousers, the gaudiest sweaters, the heaviest boots, the silliest knitted hats that ever burst from the over-charged imagination of a Winter Sports Department. The faces were pale, true, but—Henry noted with a sinking heart—quite aggressively merry and free from any sign of stress: the voices were unnaturally loud and friendly. The whole dingy place had the air of a monstrous end-of-term party.

"Will you pay the taxi, darling, while I cope with the luggage?" Emmy's amused voice recalled Henry from his fascinated appraisal of the dog beneath the Englishman's skin.

"Yes, yes, of course. No, don't try to lift it... I'll get a porter..."

The taxi grumbled on its way, and Henry was gratified to see that a small porter with the face of a malevolent monkey, who had been lounging by the wall rolling a cigarette with maddening deliberation, now came forward to offer his services.

"Santa Chiara, sir? 'Ave you got skis to register through?" The porter almost smiled.

"No," said Henry. "We're hiring them out there. We've just got—"

But the porter had abruptly lost interest, and transferred his attentions to a taxi which had just drawn up, and which most evidently had skis to register through. A man with a smooth red face and unmistakably military bearing was getting out, followed by a bristling forest of skis and sticks, and a large woman with a bad-tempered expression. As the wizened porter swept the skis and sticks expertly on to his trolley, Henry caught sight of a boldly-written label—"Col. Buckfast, Albergo Bella Vista, Santa Chiara, Italy. Via Innsbruck."

"They're at our hotel," he muttered miserably to Emmy.

She grinned. "Never mind. So are those nice youngsters over there."

Henry turned to see a group of three young people, who were certainly outstanding as far as good looks were concerned. The girl was about twenty years old, Henry judged, with short-cropped hair and brilliantly candid blue eyes. One of the young men was quite remarkably handsome, fair and grey-eyed, with very beautiful hands—at once strong and sensitive ("I've seen his picture somewhere," whispered Emmy). The other youth did not quite achieve the standard of physical perfection set by the rest of the party—he was tall and thin, with a beak of a nose and dark hair that was rather too long—but he made up for it by the dazzling appearance of his clothes. His trousers, skin-tight, were pale blue, like a Ruritanian officer's in a musical comedy: his sweater was the yellow of egg-yolks, with geranium-red reindeer circumnavigating it just below the armpits: his woollen cap, in shape like the ultimate decoration of a cream cake, was royal blue. At the moment, he was laughing uproariously, slapping a spindly blue leg with a bamboo ski-stick.

"Good heavens," said Henry. "That's Jimmy Passendell—old Raven's youngest son. He's..." He hesitated, because the idea seemed ludicrous—"...he's a member of Lloyd's."

At that moment a burly porter, evidently deciding that the time had come to clear the pavement for newcomers, seized Henry's luggage unceremoniously, tucking a suitcase under each arm and picking up the other two with effortless ease; and with a bellow of "Where to, sir?" he disappeared into the station without waiting for an answer.

Henry and Emmy trotted dutifully after him, and found themselves beside a giant weighing machine, which at the moment was laden with skis.

"Which registered?" asked the porter laconically, twirling Emmy's dressing-case playfully in his huge hand.

"I'm afraid I don't quite understand about..." Henry began, feeling almost unbearably foolish. Everybody else obviously understood.

"Registered goes straight through—Customs here—don't see it again till Innsbruck," said the porter, pityingly.

"We'll register the two big ones," said Emmy firmly.

For the next few minutes Henry trotted between luggage, porter, and ticket office like a flustered but conscientious mother bird intent on satisfying her brood's craving for worms—the worms in this case being those cryptic bits of paper which railway officials delight to stamp, perforate, clip, and shake their heads over. Eventually all was done, the Customs cleared, and Henry and Emmy were safely installed, with the two smaller cases, in the corner seats reserved for their journey to Dover.

Henry sank back with a sigh in which relief was not unmingled with apprehension. For the moment they had the carriage to themselves, and the screaming chaos of the luggage shed had given way to the sounds of muted excitement which precede the departure of a long-distance train.

"I suppose the Yard know what they're doing," said Henry. "Because I don't. I wish we'd decided to do our skiing somewhere else."

"Nonsense," said Emmy. "I'm enjoying myself. And I haven't seen anybody in the least suspicious yet, except the taxi-driver and that screwed-up porter."

Henry gave her a reproving, walls-have-ears glance, and opened his *Times*, turning gratefully to the civilised solace of the crossword puzzle.

Henry Tibbett was not a man who looked like a great detective. In fact, as he would be the first to point out, he was not a great detective, but a conscientious and observant policeman, with an occasional flair for intuitive detection which he called "my nose". There were very few of his superiors who were not prepared to listen, and to take appropriate action, when Henry said, suddenly, "My nose tells me we're on the wrong lines. Why not tackle it this way?" The actual nose in question was as pleasant—and as unremarkable—as the rest of Henry Tibbett. A small man, sandy-haired and with pale eyebrows and lashes which emphasised his general air of timidity, he had spent most of his forty-eight years trying to avoid trouble—with a conspicuous lack of success.

"It's not my fault," he once remarked plaintively to Emmy, "that things always seem to blow up at my feet." The consequence was that he had a wide and quite undeserved reputation as a desperado, an adventurer who hid his bravura under a mask of meekness: and his repeated assertions that he only wanted to lead a quiet life naturally fed the flames of this rumour.

Emmy, of course, knew Henry as he really was—and knew that the truth about him lay somewhere between the swash-buckling figure of his subordinates' imagination, and the mild and mousy character he protested himself to be. She knew, too—and it reassured and comforted her—that Henry needed her placid strength and good humour as much as he needed food and drink. She was forty now—not as slim as she had been, but with a pleasantly curving figure and a pleasantly intelligent face. Her most striking feature was her skin, which was wonderfully white and fair, a piquant contrast to her curly black hair.

She looked at her watch. "We'll be off soon" she said. "I wonder who else is in our carriage."

They very soon found out. Mrs. Buckfast's voice could be heard raised in complaint a full corridor away, before she finally entered the carriage like a man-o'-war under full sail. Her seat, naturally, was the wrong one. She had definitely been given to understand that she would have a corner seat, facing the engine.

"I can only say, Arthur," she said, her eyes fixed on Henry, "that reservations seem to mean absolutely nothing to *some people*." Unhappily, Henry offered her his seat. Mrs. Buckfast started, as though seeing him for the first time; then accepted the seat with a bad grace.

Soon a cheerful commotion in the corridor heralded the arrival of Jimmy Passendell and his party. ("Seven in a carriage is *far too many*," Mrs. Buckfast announced to nobody in particular.) The girl became engrossed in the latest copy of the *Tatler*. Colonel Buckfast nodded briefly at the handsome young man, and said, "Back again this year, eh? Had a feeling you might be." The young man remarked that he hoped the snow would be as good as it had been the year before, and proceeded to cope expertly with the baggage, even coaxing a sour smile from Mrs. Buckfast by lifting a large number of small cases up to the rack for her. Jimmy Passendell immediately counteracted this momentary lightening of the atmosphere by producing a mouth organ and inviting the company to join him in the chorus of "Dear Old Pals".

"After all," he remarked brightly, "we soon shall be—we're all going to Santa Chiara, aren't we—to the Bella Vista." After a pause, he added, "Yippee!" The pretty blonde giggled; the handsome youth looked uncomfortable; the Colonel and Henry retreated still further behind their respective *Times*; Emmy laughed outright, and produced a tin of digestive biscuits, which she offered to all and sundry. The young people fell on them with whoops of delight, and for a time conversation was mercifully replaced by a contented munching. The train moved slowly out of Victoria into the mist.

❀ ❀ ❀

The channel was grey and cold, but calm. The skiers clumped cheerfully up the gangplank in their resounding boots, and made a concerted dash for the warmth and solace of the saloon, dining-room or bar according to temperament. As the steamer moved slowly away from the dockside and out of the narrow harbour entrance, Henry and Emmy had the deck to themselves. They leant over the rail, savouring the peace, the absence of strident human voices, and watching the familiar outline of the cliffs grow dim in the haze.

"There's nobody else going to Santa Chiara," said Emmy, at last. "And none of that lot look like dope-peddlers to me, whatever other failings they may have."

"The whole thing's probably a wild goose chase," said Henry. "I hope it is. Heaven knows I don't want any trouble. I want to learn to ski. After all, we are on holiday."

"Are we?" Emmy gave him a rueful smile. "Just pure coincidence that we're going to the hotel which Interpol thinks is a smugglers' den?"

"It was just my luck to pick that particular place," said Henry, ruefully. "And when Sir John heard we were going there, I couldn't very well refuse to keep my eyes open."

"Interpol know you're going to be there, though, don't they?"

"Yes—unofficially. They've no evidence against the place as yet—only suspicions. They were thinking of sending one of their own chaps to the Bella Vista as an ordinary holiday-maker, but when Sir John told them I was going anyway—"

Behind them, a familiar voice boomed. "It was *clearly* understood that we would travel first-class on the boat..."

"Let's have a drink," said Henry, hastily, and piloted Emmy down the companionway to the bar.

It was crowded, smoky and cheerful. Henry battled his way between young giants to the counter, and secured two Scotches and two hundred cigarettes for a laughable sum. By the time he had fought his way back to Emmy, she had already installed herself in the last remaining chair in the bar, and was chatting amicably to the fair girl, whose escorts were storming the bar in search of duty-free cognac.

"Oh, well done, Henry. Come and meet Miss Whittaker." Emmy seemed for some reason to stress the surname as she said it. Heavens, thought Henry. Somebody I ought to know. The girl beamed at him.

"Miss Whittaker sounds too silly," she said. "Please call me Caro."

Henry said he would be delighted to, and gave Emmy her drink. A moment later the handsome, fair-haired young man emerged from the scrum at the bar, laden with glasses and bottles. Caro fluttered into a whirl of introductions. This was darling Roger—Roger Staines, actually—who was a *frightfully* good skier and was going to shame them all—but *shame* them— and this was Henry and Emmy Tibbett and they were going to the Bella Vista—actually to the same hotel—wasn't that too extraordinary and blissful, Roger darling? Then darling Jimmy arrived with his ration of duty-free, and the party made merry, while the grey sea-miles slipped away under the keel, and the seagulls wheeled purposefully over the writhing white wake of the ship.

Calais was a scramble of porters, a perfunctory interlude with the Customs, a trek along seeming miles of platform—and eventually all five travellers were installed in Compartment E6 of a gleaming train, which had a showy plaque reading "Skisports Special" screwed to its smoking flanks. The hand-luggage was stowed away neatly above the door, and the first bottle of brandy opened (by Jimmy). The great train heaved a spluttering sigh, and pulled smoothly out of the station, heading south.

"And here we are," said Jimmy, "until to-morrow. Have some brandy."

❀ ❀ ❀

France rolled away behind them in the already deepening dusk. Henry did his crossword; Emmy dozed; Jimmy took another swig of brandy; Caro read her magazine, and Roger stared moodily out of the window, a sulky look of bad temper ruining his impeccable profile. A small man in a leather jerkin, wearing a red armband embroidered with the words "Skisports Ltd." in yellow, put his head into the carriage.

"I'm Edward, your courier on the train," he announced brightly, blinking through thick-lensed spectacles. "Anything you want, just ask me."

"Have some brandy," said Jimmy. Edward tittered nervously, refused, and withdrew. They heard him open the door of the next compartment.

"I'm Edward, your courier on the train. If there's anything—"

"There most certainly is, my man." Mrs. Buckfast's voice rose easily above the rhythmic pulse of the wheels. They could hear it rumbling on in discontent even when the unfortunate Edward had been lured into the carriage, and the door firmly shut behind him.

A few minutes later, Caro got up and went into the corridor, where she stood leaning on the window rail, looking out at the darkening fields, the lighted farmhouse windows, the tiny country stations, as they flashed past, tossed relentlessly from future to past by the insatiable, mile-hungry monster of which they were now a part.

Emmy glanced after Caro, suddenly awake, then settled herself to sleep again. Roger Staines got up from his corner seat, and went out into the corridor, slamming the door behind him. He stood beside Caro, two backviews, inexpressive, lurching with the movement of the train. Henry could see that he was talking earnestly; that she was replying hardly at all. He could not hear what they were saying.

❈ ❈ ❈

At five o'clock the lights of the train came on suddenly, and at six-thirty the bell sounded merrily down the corridor for First Dinner. Jimmy consulted his ticket and found that he was, indeed, due to dine at the first sitting: so, collecting Roger and Caro who were now leaning relaxedly against the carriage door, smoking and chatting idly, they went off with considerable clatter down the corridor towards the dining-car.

It seemed very quiet and empty when they had gone. Henry got up and shut the door carefully. Then he said, "Roger Staines… I wish I could place him…"

"I've remembered where I've seen his picture—in the *Tatler*," said Emmy. "He's what they call a deb's delight. Look—"

She picked up the magazine that was lying on the seat where Caro had left it. It was open at one of the familiar pages which report so tirelessly on the night-life of London, and there was a photograph of Roger and Caro toasting each other in champagne. "Miss Caroline Whittaker, Sir Charles and Lady Whittaker's lovely daughter, shares a drink and a jest at the Four Hundred with her favourite escort, Mr. Roger Staines," said the caption, coyly. Henry looked at the picture for a full minute, thoughtfully. He said again, "I wish I could place him—further back. Quite a bit further back."

"Goodness, I'm hungry," said Emmy. "Have a biscuit."

The train sped on towards the frontiers of Switzerland.

❈ ❈ ❈

Henry and Emmy shared their table at Third Dinner with Colonel and Mrs. Buckfast. The latter, having obviously had the time of her life making mincemeat of poor Edward, was in a comparatively good humour, and agreed to take a glass of

Sauternes with her fish; she even pronounced the food eatable. Her husband, evidently cheered by this unaccustomed serenity, became conversational over the coffee.

"Your first time on skis?" he asked Henry, his smooth red face aglow with affability.

"Yes, I'm a complete rabbit, I'm afraid," Henry replied. "My wife's done it before."

"Only twice," said Emmy. "I'm no good at all."

"Finest sport in the world," said the Colonel. He glanced round belligerently, as if expecting instant contradiction. Mrs. Buckfast sniffed, but said nothing. "My wife doesn't ski," he added, confidentially. "Jolly sporting of her to come out with me, year after year. I appreciate it. Of course, I'd absolutely understand if she wanted to stay behind and let me go alone..." His voice took on a wistful note.

"The mountain air is good for me," said Mrs. Buckfast, flatly. "I find ways of passing the time. It really wouldn't be fair to let poor Arthur do this trip all by himself."

"I've often told you—" he began, but she cut him short with a "Pass the sugar please, Arthur," that brooked no further discussion. There was a short silence, and then the Colonel tried again.

"Been to Santa Chiara before?" he asked.

"No."

"Interested to know what attracted you, if you're not a keen skier. Not everybody's cup of tea—hotel stuck up all by itself at the top of a chair-lift. Can't get down to the village at all after dark, you know."

"They told us the skiing was excellent," said Emmy, "and we wanted peace and quiet more than anything."

"Then you certainly picked the right spot," said Mrs. Buckfast, sourly. "I dare say," she went on, with ill-concealed curiosity, "that your husband has been working very hard. Perhaps his job is a very exhausting one."

"No more so than any other business man's," said Henry. "It's just a question of temperament, I suppose. We always like quiet holidays, off the beaten track."

"So you're a business man are you? How very interesting. In the City?"

"Not exactly," said Henry. "I work in Westminster."

Mrs. Buckfast, foiled in her attempt to extract more information about Henry's profession, went on, "Quite a distinguished party going to Santa Chiara this year. Caroline Whittaker, who had that huge ball at Claridge's last year, and the Honourable Jimmy Passendell—" her voice sank to a whisper—"Lord Raven's son you know. A bit *wild*, I understand, but charming...so charming..."

"The other lad seems pleasant, too," said Henry. "Roger Staines. I seem to know his face."

"I know nothing about him," said Mrs. Buckfast, with great firmness. "*Nothing*," she added, "whatsoever."

❀ ❀ ❀

When Henry and Emmy got back to E6, the triple tiers of bunks had been set up, but the party showed no signs of going to bed. Jimmy had opened another bottle of brandy, and was leading the company in a variety of more or less bawdy songs. Henry and Emmy accepted a nightcap gratefully, and then suggested that they should retire to bed on the two top bunks, out of everyone's way. "Don't mind us old drears," said Emmy. "Sing as loud as you like. We enjoy it."

"Jolly decent of you," said Jimmy. "Have another drink before you embark on the perilous ascent." He said the last two words twice to make sure of getting them right. Caro was smiling now, sitting in the corner and holding hands with Roger.

In fact, the singing only went on for half an hour or so, before the whole party decided to get some rest. Caro took one of the two middle bunks, Roger and Jimmy the two lowest. Soon all was dark and quiet, except for the tiny blue bulb that burned in the ceiling, the soft breathing of the sleepers, and the thrumming wheels on the ribbon-stretch of rails. In his tiny compartment at the rear of the last coach, Edward cursed

Mrs. Buckfast steadily, and with satisfaction, as he compiled his passenger list: between him and the engine driver, the sinuous length of train was all asleep.

At breakfast time next morning they were miraculously among mountains. True, the railway itself ran through wide, flat green valleys, like the beds of dried-up lakes, but all around the mountains reared proudly, fresh green giving way to grey rock, to evergreen, and finally, high above, to glistening white snow. All along the train, voices and spirits rose. The sun shone, and the snow, suddenly real, suddenly remembered, was a lure, a liberator, a potent magic. Soon, soon...

The Austrian border was left behind at half-past nine: by eleven the train was winding along the broad green valley of the River Inn, ringed by lofty mountains: at eleven-twenty precisely, the engine drew to a hissing, panting halt, and a guttural voice outside on the platform was shouting "Innsbruck! Innsbruck!" into the crisp, sunny air.

# Chapter Two

At Innsbruck, the compact phalanx of skiers who had travelled *en masse* from Victoria dispersed abruptly: hotel buses or small, energetic mountain trains bore them off to their respective Austrian resorts. Only the Santa Chiara party remained, suddenly rather desolate, suddenly rather out of place in their aggressive sweaters. Edward, who had come in for some uncomplimentary remarks from E6 on the train, now seemed like their last—and faithless—friend, as he hurriedly compiled his reports, and headed for his overnight lodgings in Innsbruck.

Inevitably the camaraderie of isolation manifested itself. Jimmy fetched a cup of coffee for Mrs. Buckfast, the Colonel carried Emmy's overnight case up the subway for her, Roger (with a superior command of German) collected the registered baggage, and Emmy and Caro ventured together in search of the Ladies'. Henry, feeling rather out of things, contented himself with buying enough English magazines at the bookstall to keep the whole party happy until teatime, when they were due at their destination.

Eventually all seven travellers, complete with luggage, were assembled on the correct platform to catch the Munich-

Rome express, which was to carry them on the penultimate stage of their journey.

Evidently not many people wanted to exchange the exhilarating sunshine of Innsbruck for the uncertain joys of Rome in January, for nobody else was waiting for the train except an elderly couple who, Henry guessed, had been marketing in Innsbruck and were probably going no farther than Brenner, the frontier town. A few minutes before the train was due, however, a flurry of porters and expensive luggage appeared from the subway, followed by a tall and very thin man, dressed in a sort of Norfolk jacket made of bright green tweed, with a fur collar, and dark grey trousers of extreme narrowness. His face was long, and creased with deep lines of intolerance, and his lean, vulpine features were crowned incongruously by a green Tyrolean hat. With him was a girl of striking beauty: she had the face of a Florentine Madonna, with deep golden hair swept smoothly back from a broad brow and coiled on the nape of her neck. She wore pale grey ski trousers cut by a master, and a little grey jacket with a collar of snow leopard that framed her face like a cloud. Her make-up—in the Italian manner—emphasised her magnificent dark eyes, and her honey-coloured skin, while her full, lovely mouth was brushed lightly with a wild-rose pink. "Very, very expensive," Emmy whispered to Henry, as the procession of porters swept past.

Mrs. Buckfast gazed after the newcomers with uninhibited curiosity: Caro looked sheepish, suddenly conscious of her crumpled, slept-in trousers: the men, involuntarily, turned to admire, and were rewarded by a scowl from under the Tyrolean hat.

When the train pulled in, dead on time, and they had secured an empty carriage for the party without difficulty, Henry and Emmy went to the window to take a last look at Innsbruck. To their surprise, Tyrolean Hat was on the platform alone, obviously saying goodbye to the Madonna, who stood, cool and beautiful, at the window of a first-class compartment. There were kisses, protestations of affection, fussings over baggage—all of which the girl received with what looked more like dutiful resignation than enthusiasm. At one point, when the man was engaged in some sort of altercation with the porter, Henry caught her looking at him with an expression of mingled contempt and dislike which was chilling in its intensity. At last the whistle blew, and the train started. The last view of Innsbruck was of a Tyrolean hat waving, somehow pathetically, on the end of a long, thin arm.

❀ ❀ ❀

At Brenner, after a short and amicable interlude with the Italian Customs, the whole party filed down the corridor to the dining-car. The young people secured a table for four, and the Buckfasts a table for two: Henry and Emmy, arriving last, were ushered by a smiling waiter to the last table in the car—a four-seater at present occupied by one person only, the Madonna from Innsbruck. She was ordering her meal in fluent Italian, completely relaxed, spontaneous and excited—a very different person from the cool beauty of Innsbruck station. "Like a little girl out of school," Henry thought.

Throughout a delectable meal that started with *fettuccini* and meandered through *fritto misto con fagiolini* to a creamy *bel paese* cheese, there was more concentration on food than on conversation. With the coffee, however, a pleasantly replete and relaxed mood took over; the beauty made the first move by inquiring in excellent English whether Henry and Emmy were from London, and were they holidaying in Italy? They said they were.

"So am I," she said, with a ravishing smile of pure happiness. "I am Italian, you see. But my husband is Austrian, and there we must live, in Innsbruck."

"I envy you," said Henry. "It must be a beautiful city."

"Yes," said the girl, shortly. Then, smiling again—"But where do you go? Rome? Venezia? Firenze?"

"As a matter of fact, we're going to ski," said Emmy.

"Oh! I too."

"Perhaps we might even be headed for the same place," Henry suggested.

"I am sure we are not," said the beauty. "You go to Cortina, of course. All English and Americans go to Cortina."

"No," said Henry. "We're going to a little place called Santa Chiara. The Albergo Bella Vista."

To his surprise, the girl's smile faded abruptly, and for an instant a look of sheer panic crossed her face.

"Santa Chiara," she said, almost in a whisper. "I...I go there, too."

"Well how nice," said Emmy, quickly. "We must introduce ourselves. We are Henry and Emmy Tibbett."

"And I..." There was an unmistakable hesitation. Then the girl seemed to shake herself, like a puppy coming out of the sea, and her smile flashed again. "I am the Baroness von Wurtburg. But you must call me Maria-Pia. When I am in Italy, I forget that I have become an Austrian."

There was a tiny pause.

"My children are already at the Bella Vista, with the fraulein," the Baroness went on. "Hansi is eight, and Lotte six. You will meet them."

"I'll look forward to that," said Emmy, suppressing her instinct to remark that the Baroness looked ridiculously young to have an eight-year-old son. "What a pity," she added, daringly, "that your husband can't be with you, too."

Once again the panic flickered in the huge, brown eyes. "He is very busy, he cannot get away. He lets me—I mean, he likes me to return to my country each year, but he does not love Italy."

"I bet he doesn't," thought Henry, remembering the harsh features under the Tyrolean hat. He felt very sorry for the Baroness and did not know how to convey his sympathy without seeming impertinent: so he quickly paid his bill and, with friendly assurances that they would meet again soon, ushered Emmy down the dining-car. As they went, Henry felt, curiously, those magnificent eyes following him. At the door he turned, to meet the Baroness's quiet, quizzical gaze. She looked him full in the eyes, and raised her head very slightly, as if in defiance. Henry, somewhat embarrassed, smiled and stepped into the swaying corridor.

At Chiusa, they made their last change. The great express rushed on southwards towards Verona, leaving the nine travellers standing in the sunshine on the little country station. All round them, the Dolomites broke the skyline with their warm, pink summits—flat rocks, pinnacled rocks, shapes whittled by wind and snow into primeval patterns of frightening strength and durability; the strength of the very old, the very tough, that has endured and will endure for time beyond thinking.

From the majesty of the mountains, a shrill tooting brought the party back to reality. There, on the opposite line, stood the most endearing train in the world. The engine—tiny, of 1870s vintage, with a tall, slender chimney and gleaming brasswork—headed just two coaches made of pale, fretted woodwork, with elaborate iron-railed observation platforms at each end. The Gothic windows of one carriage were chintz-curtained, marking them as First Class. The seats throughout were of slatted wood, with overhead racks for skis.

The young English exclaimed with delight, and made a concerted scramble for the train with their cases, closely followed by Henry and Emmy. Mrs. Buckfast remarked that it was high time they put new coaches on this line—the wooden seats were a disgrace. The Baroness, with every porter in the place at her heels, walked slowly across the flat railway track with an expression of pure love on her face. The luggage was loaded, the train shrilled its whistle, and the last lap of the journey began.

As the crow flies, it is about twenty miles from Chiusa to Santa Chiara: as the railway line winds, it is over thirty—thirty miles of tortuous, twisting track, of hairpin bends on the edge of precipices, of Stygian, smoky tunnels, of one-in-five gradients, and of some of the most breathtaking views in the world. Almost at once, they crossed the snowline, among pine trees. Soon

Chiusa was just a huddle of pink and ochre houses far below. Valleys opened out gloriously, houses lost their Italianate look and became steadily more and more Alpine, with wooden balconies and eyebrows of snow on their steep, overhanging eaves. Up and up the engine puffed and snorted, nearer and nearer to the snowfields and the pink peaks. At village halts, white-aproned peasant women clambered on and off the train with baskets of eggs and precious green vegetables. Then they saw the first of the skiers. Round a steep bend, a glistening nursery slope opened up alongside the railway line, peopled with tiny, speeding figures. Excitement rose, like yeast. Up and up the train climbed, through three small resort villages, until at last a pink, onion-domed church came into view, clustered about with little houses.

"Santa Chiara," said the Baroness.

They all craned to look. The village was set at the head of a long valley—a valley of which the floor itself was over 5,000 feet above sea-level. All round, the mountains stood in a semicircle, at once protective and menacing. The village seemed very small and very brave, up there in the white heights.

There was not, strictly speaking, a station. The train, showing signs of exhaustion, clanked and rumbled to a halt in the middle of a snowfield near the church: here, by a small green-painted shed, several hotel porters waited with their big luggage sledges, while skiers returning to the village for tea zoomed in an uninhibited manner across the railway line.

As the Baroness got out of the train, there was a sudden flurry as two diminutive skiers hurtled down the slope, crossed the railway tracks, and swung round in perfect parallel cristiania turns to stop dead in a spray-shower of snow beside the train.

"Mamma! Mamma!" they yelled, and the Baroness dropped her white pigskin dressing-case in the snow and rushed to embrace them. The reunion was noisy, sentimental and rather moving: it was not for several moments that Henry noticed a slender, dark girl in black who had skied quietly but extremely competently down to the train behind the children, and now stood a few paces away, silently watching the out-pourings of affection. She was very pale, in sharp contrast to the bronzed faces all round her, and she wore no make-up. She might have been beautiful, Henry thought, had she taken even the most elementary steps to make herself so: as it was, she seemed to concentrate on self-effacement, on anonymity.

The first greetings over, the Baroness—one arm round each of her children—beamed at the dark girl and spoke to her in German. Then she said to Emmy, "I go now with Gerda and the children for tea. The porter will take you up to the Bella Vista, so I shall see you at dinner."

She gave instructions in rapid Italian to a burly porter who had "Bella Vista" embroidered in gold on his black cap, and then, as the children skied slowly down the hill to the village street, she ran after them, laughing and teasing, trying to keep up with them. The dark-haired Gerda let them get near the bottom of the slope, then launched herself forward with a lovely, fluid movement, and took the gentle hillside in a series of superbly-executed turns, gathering speed all the way, so that she was waiting for the others at the bottom, as still and silent as before.

As the porter loaded the baggage on to his sledge, Colonel Buckfast spoke for the first time that Henry could remember since Innsbruck.

"Look," he said, pointing upwards.

They all looked. Behind the railway line, the mountains reared in white splendour: by now, the sun had left the village, but lingered on the rosy peaks and on the high snowfields. Far up the mountain, where the trees thinned out, just on the dividing line between sunshine and shadow, was a single, isolated building, as dwarfed by its surroundings as a fly drowning in a churn of milk.

"The Bella Vista," said the Colonel, almost reverently.

There was a silence.

"I didn't realise it was so far up," said Emmy at last, in a small voice. "How do we get there?"

"We get there," said Mrs. Buckfast, "in a diabolical contraption known as a chair-lift. Every year I say I'll never do it again, and every year Arthur talks me into it. The very thought of it makes me feel sick. This way."

The Monte Caccia chair-lift, as all the brochures emphasise, is one of the longest in Europe. The ascent takes twenty-five minutes, during which time the chairs, on their stout overhead cable, travel smoothly and safely upwards, sometimes over steep slopes between pine trees, a mere twenty feet from the ground, more frequently over gorges and ravines which twist and tumble several hundred feet below. About once a minute, the strong metal arm which connects the chair to the cable clatters and bumps as it passes between the platforms of a massive steel pylon, set on four great concrete bases and equipped with a fire-broom and a sturdy snow-shovel in case of emergencies. For parts of the trip, the lift travels above the *pistes*, or ski runs, giving the passengers a bird's-eye view of the expertise or otherwise of the skiers below. It is one of the coldest forms of travelling known to man.

Henry was amused to see the varying reactions of the party (including himself) when faced with this ascent—especially when the first-timers grasped the fact that the chairs did not stop at any point, but continued up and down on an endless belt, so that one had to "hop" a moving chair as it passed.

The Colonel slid expertly into his chair, and waved his hand from sheer exhilaration as he soared skywards: Mrs. Buckfast took her seat competently, but with resignation, having grudgingly accepted the bright red blanket proffered by the attendant. Caro, glancing at the seemingly endless cables stretching up the mountainside, turned rather pale and remarked that she hadn't imagined it would be quite like this, and that heights made her dizzy.

"Don't worry, you'll get used to it in no time," said Roger, briskly. "There's absolutely nothing to be frightened of. I'll be in the chair right behind you. Just put down the safety-bar, and then relax and enjoy the view."

Caro showed no signs of enjoying herself, but she got on to the next seat without further demur, clutching a little desperately at the vertical metal arm, like a nervous child on a roundabout, as the chair sped upwards. Roger exchanged a joke in Italian with the attendant, and had time to discover that his name was Carlo and that the lift stopped working at seven o'clock each evening, before he slipped casually into his chair, leaving the safety arm flapping. Jimmy made a loudly facetious remark about dicing with death, which made Henry suspect that he was genuinely apprehensive, but he hopped his chair gamely enough, the neck of a brandy bottle protruding from his hip pocket. It seemed to Henry that he had had to wait an eternity for his turn, but in fact the chairs came round so rapidly that it was less than a minute after the Colonel had boarded the lift that Henry—only partly reassured by Emmy's encouraging smile—found himself waiting in the appointed spot for the next down-travelling chair to complete its circuit by clanking round the huge wheel in the shed; a couple of seconds later it came up and hit him in the back of the knees. He sat down, and the ascent began.

The ride up to the Bella Vista was certainly cold: and over some of the more precipitous ravines Henry found it advisable to keep his eyes focused stubbornly on the heights to come, rather than glancing down to the huddled, snowy rocks below. But there was a magic, too, in the slow, steady, silent ascent—silent, that is, apart from the clatter and rattle each time the chair passed a pylon: and yet the unnerving effect of this noise was counteracted by a momentary sense of security, for the inspection platform of the pylon passed a mere eighteen inches below his dangling feet, and, noticing that a steel ladder led down from the platform to the ground below, Henry hoped fervently that if the lift did decide to break down, it would do so when he was passing a pylon, rather than at a moment when he was suspended over a precipitous gorge.

To the right, about ten feet away, was the downward cable of the lift, on which a procession of empty seats followed each other towards the valley with the stately melancholy of a deserted merry-go-round. Just occasionally, however, a down-going chair was occupied—generally by a booted and be-furred lady of uncertain years. It was very much, Henry reflected, like being on an escalator in the London underground, watching the faces that glided downwards as one ascended, to come face to face and level for a fleeting moment before the inexorable machinery churned on. When it came to scenery, however, all resemblance disappeared. Instead of the garish rectangles of advertisement which London Transport provides for the entertainment of its passengers, there were vistas of snow, cloud and mountain, of pine trees and pink rock, of misty valleys and sun-touched peaks. At last, a tiny hut came into view at the top of an open snowfield—the trees were all but left behind. As the chair approached, a little wizened man with a walnut-brown face stood ready to take Henry's arm and help him as he slid maladroitly out of the chair before it clattered on round the wheel to begin its descent.

Emmy came sailing up serenely on the next chair, slipped gracefully out of it, and came over to stand beside Henry.

"Well," she said, "here we are. And isn't it wonderful?"

Far, far below them, Santa Chiara looked like a toy village laid out on a nursery floor, the minuscule houses dotted haphazardly round the apricot-pink church. Ahead, over the ridge where the ski-lift ended, a shallow, saucer-shaped sweep of snowfields stretched away to still more mountain peaks; and to the right, round the bend of a snow-banked path, was the Albergo Bella Vista. The rest of the party were already walking up the path to the hotel, stopping every few yards to draw each other's attention to some fresh beauty. Henry and Emmy followed them slowly, hand in hand and very much at peace.

# Chapter Three

O
ne of the charms of mountain architecture is its consistency.
The deep eaves and steep roof-tops, the wooden balconies and
shuttered windows, have been universal above a certain altitude
for centuries—simply because they are functional, providing the
greatest comfort and security for men living among the snows.
So the Albergo Bella Vista looked exactly like any other mountain chalet, with its neat mosaic of stacked firewood nudging
one wall, its balcony-veranda and pale wooden shutters pierced
with heart-shaped holes.

In the hall—floors and walls of honey-coloured waxed
pine—a man in a light blue suit, plump as a capon and with
sparse grey hair trained carefully to hide his pink baldness, was
oozing welcome.

"Allow me to present myself... Rossati, Alberto...welcome
to the Bella Vista, *meine Herrschaften*...ah, welcome back Colonel
Buckfast...Herr Staines...if you would kindly sign the register...
this way, *bitteschoen*...may I have your passports, please..."

One by one the travellers signed in, surrendered passports, were allotted keys. By this time the luggage had
arrived, having made the ascent on one of the two tray-

shaped luggage-carriers attached to the chair-lift. At last all was sorted out, and Henry and Emmy found themselves alone in their bedroom. It was of light wood, like the rest of the building—the floor bare of carpets, yet warm to the touch, for an enormous radiator shimmered heat from below the window. The big intricately-carved bed had, in place of blankets, two vast white downy quilts, a foot thick and light as thistledown. A very large wardrobe, a plain deal dressing-table, a wash-basin and two upright chairs completed the furniture.

An exchange in Italian with the chambermaid elicited the information that a bath was certainly available, at the price of 500 lire.

"That's more than five shillings," said Henry, outraged.

"Baths are always a terrible price in the mountains," said Emmy, cheerfully. "I never reckon on having more than one a week. But just at the moment I think it would be cheap at a pound."

So they bathed luxuriously, and changed into clean clothes, and by a quarter to seven were ready to face the world and an apéritif.

The bar ran the whole length of the building, one side of it being composed entirely of windows, which gave on to the veranda. It was dark outside, for the moon was not yet up, but still the snow glimmered faintly white below the ink-black sky. The furniture consisted of little tables covered in red gingham table-cloths, milk-white wooden chairs, and a long chromium bar with stools upholstered in deep red leather. On the bar, inevitably, an Espresso machine hissed and wheezed like a cauldron of snakes. Henry and Emmy perched themselves on stools, and a dark, smiling girl served them with Campari-sodas. There was only one other customer in the bar—a man who sat at a table in the farthest corner and toyed with a glass of tomato-juice.

Indicating the stranger with the tiniest nod of her head, Emmy whispered, "Doesn't look like a skiing type to me."

Henry half-turned to look. He saw a small, smooth man in his fifties: everything about him was chubby, from his fat little fingers caressing the stem of his glass to his short, stumpy feet, whose outline could not be disguised by his tapering suede shoes. His face was pink, round and benevolent, with small eyes that twinkled obscurely behind thick-lensed spectacles.

After a minute or so Signor Rossati, the proprietor, came into the bar. He went quickly over to the man in the corner, and spoke to him quietly in German. The man nodded amiably, finished his drink, and the two went out together, deep in conversation. They crossed the hall and Henry heard the door of Rossati's private office click shut, cutting off the voices.

"Our host seems to be bilingual," Emmy remarked.

"Nearly everyone is, in these parts," Henry replied. "We're only just over the Austrian border, you know, and this province was part of Austria until 1919. Italian is the official language now, but German comes far more naturally to a lot of the people—especially in the smaller villages."

"Does it rankle at all, I wonder—being handed over arbitrarily to Italy?" asked Emmy.

"Officially, no. Unofficially—yes, of course. But strictly under the surface. Nothing must upset the tourist trade." Henry turned to the barmaid. "Do you speak English—*parla Inglese?*" he asked.

She giggled, shook her head, and said she didn't.

"*Tedeschi?*"

Her face lit up. "*Ja, ja.*" A quick stream of German followed, but Henry just smiled and shook his head negatively. To Emmy, he said, "You see? I'm not letting on I understand her, because I don't want our English chums to know I speak German or Italian. But you heard what she said?"

"She went too fast for me," said Emmy. "My German isn't all that good, you know. The best that can be said for it is that it's better than my Italian,"

"Well," said Henry, "she was saying that German was her mother-tongue, and she'd be delighted to speak it with us since we don't know Italian. It would be quite a relief, she said."

Suddenly the hall outside became shrill with a babble of Italian voices and a cheerful stamping of boots.

"The *sci*-lift...finish..." said the barmaid.

Through the open door, Henry saw the Baroness following Gerda and the children upstairs. A man's voice said, "Maria-Pia..." and she stopped, letting the others go on ahead of her. A dark young Italian, in extremely elegant royal blue ski-trousers, moved into Henry's line of vision. He stood at the foot of the staircase, and placed a hand on the Baroness's arm, restraining her, and talking urgently but softly. Gently, she freed her arm, shaking her head, but he caught her hand in his, pulling her down the stairs towards him. At that moment, Gerda reappeared round the bend of the staircase, her pale face impassive. Abruptly, the young man released the Baroness's hand, made some laughing remark, and ran upstairs past the two women, taking the steps two at a time. Gerda said something to the Baroness and they walked upstairs together. Meanwhile, Henry was amazed to see Colonel Buckfast and Roger Staines come in, dressed in full skiing regalia, their boots caked in snow.

"*Signori Inglesi*...very much *sci*...already to-day..." said the barmaid, trying hard. "Co-lon-el Back-fist, he *sci molto*...you not *sci*?"

"Not yet," said Henry.

"There's a nasty, icy side-slip halfway down Run Three," the Colonel was saying, in the hall. "Sensible of you to stick to Number One."

"I'm taking Run Three first thing in the morning," said Roger, defensively. "I just thought the light was a bit tricky for it this evening."

"Very wise. Never run before you can walk," said the Colonel, maddeningly. Then, in a lower tone, he added, "That cove Fritz Hauser is here again. Remember him? I saw him in Rossati's office as I went out. Don't like the fellow."

"Hauser? Oh yes, the fat little German...was here last year...can't think why he comes when he doesn't ski..."

They went upstairs.

❉ ❉ ❉

Dinner started gaily enough. The Baroness, ravishing in black velvet trousers and a white silk shirt, sat alone—but talked merrily and loudly to the dark young Italian, who also had a table to himself. Gerda, presumably, took her dinner upstairs with the children, for there was no sign of her. The Buckfasts (Mrs. Buckfast resplendent in lilac crêpe) made quite a thing about their "usual" table, which was no different from any other, but somehow established seniority. Henry and Emmy, at Jimmy's expansive invitation, joined up with the three young English at a large table in the middle of the room. The other diners were an unmistakably German family—a comfortably plump, blonde woman in her forties, an upright, sallow-faced man with a deep scar on his cheek, and a buxom girl, presumably their daughter, who wore no make-up, had her hair twisted into unbecoming ear-phone plaits, and never spoke a word. At a table in the corner, Fritz Hauser ate alone, rapidly and with serious concentration.

Roger was full of his first run of the season.

"The snow's still difficult," he announced, pontifically. "Not quite enough of it, unfortunately—it was far better this time last year. Still, it's quite simple if you know how to manage it."

"I for one certainly don't," said Henry. "I intend to enrol in the ski school first thing to-morrow morning."

There was a chime of agreement from Jimmy and Caro.

"I'll come along with you," boomed Colonel Buckfast from his table, not to be outdone by Roger. "Just to introduce you, of course. I know them all down there. Splendid lot of chaps. You want to get Giulio, if you can. Best instructor in the place. Failing him, his brother Pietro. They're the sons of old Mario, you know—man who works the top end of the chair-lift. Used to be the star instructor himself until he crocked himself up."

The Colonel settled back in his chair with a comfortable affability, delighted at having established his claim to local knowledge.

Before anybody else could speak, the Baroness said quietly, "Giulio is dead."

"What!" Roger dropped his spoon into his soup plate with a clatter, swinging round to look at the Baroness. Then, conscious that his own party were staring at him, he muttered, "I mean, I knew him quite well. He taught me when I was here last year."

"I say—I'm damned sorry to hear that," said the Colonel, who had turned a deep raspberry red. He looked genuinely distressed, but whether on account of Giulio's death, or because somebody else had found out about it before he had, Henry could not be certain.

"How did it happen, eh?" the Colonel went on. "He was only a lad."

"It was a skiing accident, so they told me in the village," said the Baroness. After a pause, she added: "Last week."

"He was a young man of great...great foolishness." The dark young Italian joined in, speaking very earnestly, partly from deep sincerity and partly because he found English difficult. "This was not surprise. If not ski...then that so-rapid automobile he drive...no chains...he must die."

"He was on the Immenfeld run, just over the Austrian border," the Baroness went on. "It's very dangerous terrain there, and the run was definitely prohibited because of the snow conditions. But just because it was forbidden, Giulio must attempt it. He was like that. They found him at the bottom of a crevasse. One ski was still on his foot. The other ski and his sticks they never found."

There was an awkward pause.

"Poor old Mario," said the Colonel at last, wiping his moustache with his napkin.

There was a clatter of wood on wood as Fritz Hauser got up and replaced his chair neatly at his table. Only he and the

German family seemed quite unmoved by the conversation. "They probably don't understand English," thought Emmy.

Hauser stopped at the Germans' table, said something in a low voice to the girl, and crossed the room to the door. There he paused, as if taking a decision. Then he turned and said in good English to the room in general: "This idiot Giulio is dead. So—it is his own fault. He disobeyed orders. Let it not be a discouragement to other skiers." He gave a curious little bow, and walked out.

"What a vile little man," said Caro.

"Yet it is true what he was saying," said the Baroness. "There is nothing to fear if one is sensible. Only the foolish come to grief."

"That's what I always say." Mrs. Buckfast spoke firmly and surprisingly. "You just have to be a little careful." All at once, Henry had an extraordinary impression of tension, as if each remark had more than its surface meaning, as if purposeful streams of innuendo were being directed by the speakers towards—whom? Everybody? One other person? He glanced round. Caro was looking uncomfortable, her eyes on her plate. Roger had pushed his food away, and seemed really distressed. The Colonel brooded, chin on chest. As quickly as it had come, the impression faded, became ridiculous. The Baroness remarked that it was a great tragedy, but that these things happened, and they mustn't let it spoil their holiday. She added that since the ice had now been broken, she'd like to introduce them all to Franco di Santi—the dark young Italian—who was a sculptor from Rome, whom she had met here on a previous visit. "So we are old friends," she added, with a dazzling smile.

This restored the conversation to normal, and when they had all professed themselves delighted to know Franco, Roger asked the Colonel pointedly if he intended to try the Gully— which was, as he explained to the others, the most direct but also the most precipitous route from the hotel to the village. The Colonel answered tartly that he had made enquiries about it, and that the *piste* was closed until further notice, owing to the extremely dangerous state of the run. Fearing that this might lead the conversation back to Giulio's foolhardiness, Emmy asked Roger how the residents of the Bella Vista generally spent their evenings, isolated as they were. Roger brightened up and said there was a damn good radiogram in the bar, and why didn't they all go and dance?

"What about that poor little German wretch," said Jimmy *sotto voce*, indicating the other table. "Let's ask her to join us."

"Yes, let's," said Caro, in a stage whisper. "The poor thing looks too bullied for words."

Henry hoped for politeness' sake that the German family did not understand English: certainly they gave no sign of knowing that they were being talked about, but continued to plough stolidly through monoliths of cheese and dishes of gherkins.

"You ask her, Roger old dear," said Jimmy. "You're the expert in Hun-talk."

"Yes, go on, Roger darling," said Caro.

With some reluctance, Roger got up and went over to the other table. They saw him exerting his not inconsiderable charm as he proffered the invitation: his reception, however, was quite brutally abrupt. Before the girl could say a word, her father rasped out a curt refusal, and all three got to their feet and stumped out of the dining-room. Roger returned to the table looking crestfallen and angry.

"Charming, I must say," he remarked, dropping into his chair again.

"What did he say, the old pig?" asked Caro, solicitously.

"Just bellowed that it was out of the question, and dragged the poor kid off before she could open her mouth," Roger answered.

"A maiden in distress...how splendid." Jimmy was enjoying himself, and his conspiratorial glee was infectious. "We must rescue her from the dragon's clutches. Who knows where her room is?"

Caro volunteered that she had seen the girl coming out of the room opposite hers on the top floor. "And my room's at the back," she added, "so hers must be over the front door."

"All right then," said Jimmy. "We'll wait until they've all gone to bed, and then Roger and I will climb up to her balcony and serenade her—"

"Don't be silly, everyone would hear you," objected Caro.

"We'll serenade her very quietly," said Jimmy a little severely. "Then she can leave a bolster in her bed and creep downstairs…"

Still plotting delightedly, they all adjourned to the bar. "… and if that old bastard comes down and makes a scene," Jimmy was saying, "I promise you I'll—"

He stopped abruptly. From the bar came the strains of a sentimental Neapolitan love song, recorded by a lush tenor to an accompaniment of dreamy guitars: and through the open door they could see the persecuted damsel waltzing sedately with Fritz Hauser, while her parents sipped coffee and Italian brandy at a table.

Emmy burst out laughing. "So much for your maiden in distress," she said.

Poor Jimmy came in for a lot of good-natured teasing, which he took with his usual equanimity. Soon they were all dancing. The Baroness danced once with Roger and several times with Franco, and then said she was exhausted and wanted to be up early next morning to ski. Soon after she had gone, Henry and Emmy decided that they, too, were ready for bed, and Franco agreed with them. When they left, Roger and Caro were demonstrating the cha-cha-cha to Jimmy, while Colonel Buckfast ordered just one more brandy, positively the last to-night, and Mrs. Buckfast complained that the Italians would never learn to make good English coffee.

Lying in bed, Emmy reached out a hand to put out the light, and said, "Poor Jimmy. His Sir Galahad act fell a little flat."

"Yes." Henry's voice was heavy with sleep. "Still, who knows…he may need it again one of these days…"

Emmy raised herself on one elbow. "You mean she wasn't enjoying herself with Hauser?"

"Well, would you?"

"I don't know. He seems quite a reasonable little fellow. Henry—"

"Mm." Henry was almost asleep.

"Henry, do you think the Baroness came here for a secret assignation with Franco di Santi? He's terribly good-looking, and I'm certain he's in love with her…"

"Oh, go to sleep," muttered Henry into his pillow.

In the silence that followed, the sound of the gramophone drifted up faintly to them, rhythmic and cloying. Emmy's last waking thought was of the unknown young man, Giulio, lying frozen and alone at the bottom of the ravine, with one ski still strapped to his foot.